The First Five Years
Port Hedland 1965-1970

Also by Stephen Outram

Books:
Wedding Speeches
Dealers: Buying, Selling & Making Money
Public Speaking: Beyond Fear
Advanced Speaking Concepts
There's No Sex in Golf
Life After

Will Public Speaking Be The Death of You? (OOP)

Blog & Articles:
stephenoutram.com

The First Five Years
Port Hedland 1965-1970

By Stephen Outram

Disclaimer: While this work is presented as fiction, it's based upon a true story, and every effort has been made to accurately describe the included events and detail; though with the vagaries of history and memory there may be inconsistencies and errors. People's names who appear in this book have not been changed and represent real people who lived at the time; street names, places, businesses, etc. also are faithful to the period.

Author: Stephen Outram

Date Published: February 1, 2014

ISBN: 978-0-9802927-9-4

Publisher: What Else is Possible?
PO Box 1770, Broadbeach, QLD. 4218. Australia

Illustrations by Stephen Outram
Photographs by Trevor Outram

Dedication

For my family

Thank you for you, and your contribution to me in this life; I am very grateful:

Trevor Outram

Molly Edwards

Karen Gay

and Candy

With special thanks to Simone Phillips.

Western Australia

A

• Port Hedland

• Canarvon

Western
Australia

Perth •

Port Agusta

Mackay •

Gold Coast •

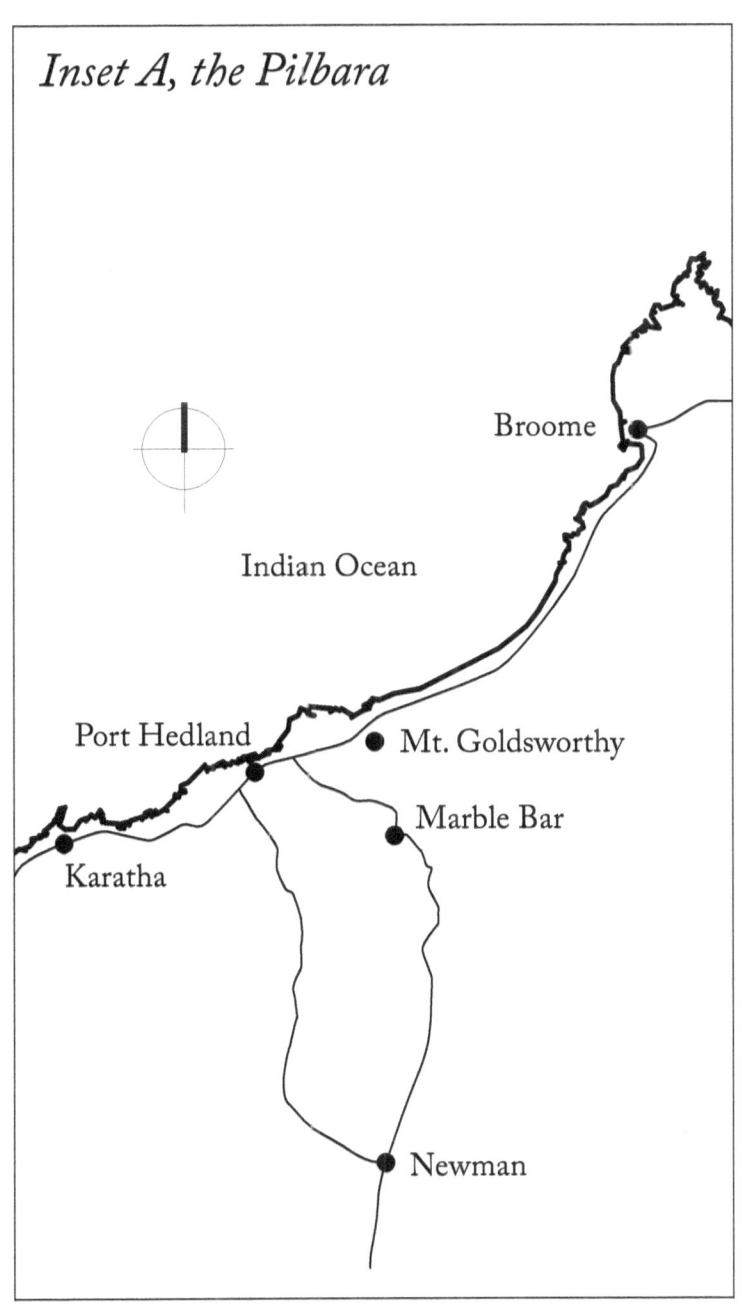

Inset A, the Pilbara

Broome

Indian Ocean

Port Hedland

Mt. Goldsworthy

Marble Bar

Karatha

Newman

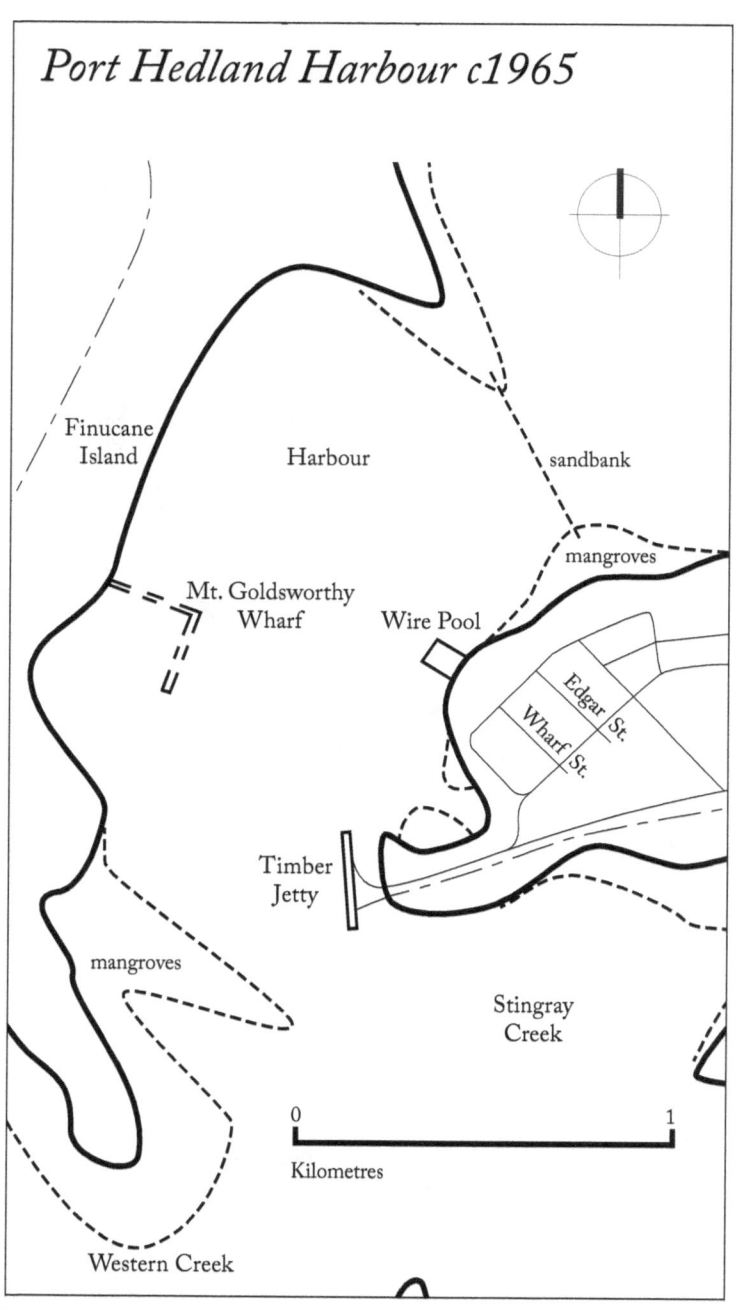

Port Hedland Harbour c1965

Finucane
Island

Harbour

sandbank

mangroves

Mt. Goldsworthy
Wharf

Wire Pool

Edgar St.

Wharf St.

Timber
Jetty

mangroves

Stingray
Creek

0   1
Kilometres

Western Creek

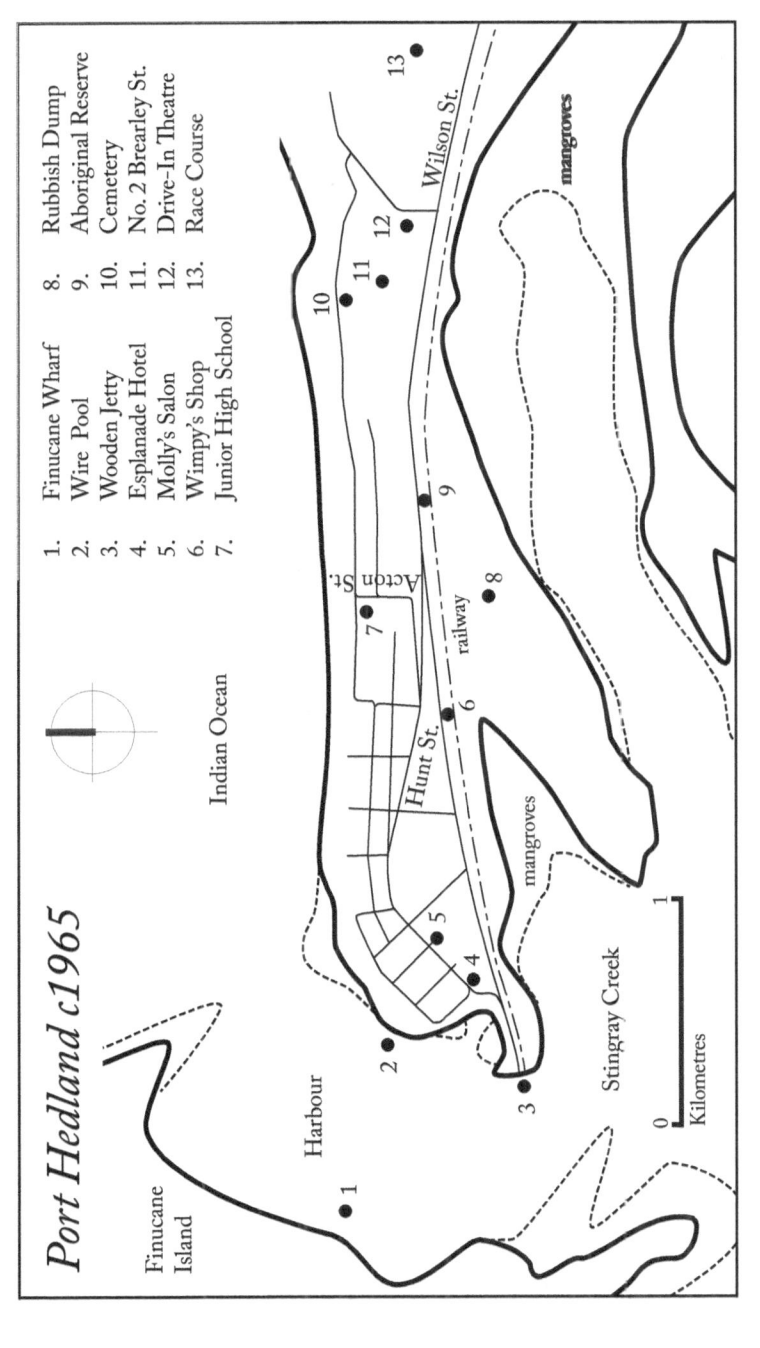

Port Hedland c1965

Finucane Island

Indian Ocean

Harbour

Stingray Creek

mangroves

mangroves

Hunt St.

Acton St.

railway

Wilson St.

1. Finucane Wharf
2. Wire Pool
3. Wooden Jetty
4. Esplanade Hotel
5. Molly's Salon
6. Wimpy's Shop
7. Junior High School
8. Rubbish Dump
9. Aboriginal Reserve
10. Cemetery
11. No. 2 Brearley St.
12. Drive-In Theatre
13. Race Course

0 1
Kilometres

Contents

Preface

Intrepid, Gutsy Pioneers

This book is based upon a true story documented in Trevor Reginald Outram's memoirs; a handwritten account of the Outram Family's immigration to Australia in 1964, covering events up until 1970.

My name is Stephen Outram and I'm Trevor's son. At age fifty seven I began adding my own recollections, from the perspective of an eight year old boy, to my Dad's work. These two different views have combined to create a unique, compelling and until now, untold adventure.

Trevor and his wife Molly immigrated to Australia with their two young children, Stephen and Karen. Their sea journey from England covered over twenty thousand kilometers, took twenty eight days to complete and landed them in Fremantle, Western Australia on January 22, 1965, amidst a record heat wave. From Perth, they travelled a further one thousand six hundred kilometers north to the remote and fledgeling town of Port Hedland, which was just beginning to boom as a port exporting iron ore from the Pilbara region of the great western state.

The family lived in Port Headland for five years before leaving in the winter of 1969.

In 1965 there was no radio, no television, no fresh milk and limited fresh fruit and vegetables in Port Hedland. It was hot, dry, remote and in complete contrast to the family's lush, green English origins. None of this was going to stop my Dad, and he set-to providing for us and creating a life in Australia, knowing that there was no supporting family and no one to fall back on; all of our immediate and extended family were thousands of kilometers away in England.

While a large portion of British immigrants, known locally as "Ten Pound Poms," chose to live in the seeming comfort of Australia's capital cities, my parent's choice of Port Hedland presented many difficulties and often extreme challenges but offered the greatest rewards. Their story is one of courage, endeavour and success; they are one of Australia's largely unknown but intrepid, gutsy pioneers.

In addition to this written work, there is a comprehensive archive of Trevor and Molly's photographs and slides that faithfully document their story. Further, in 1996 I wrote and recorded a song entitled *We've Come So Far*, which celebrates the family's journey.

The First Five Years is a terrific story and I do hope that you enjoy reading it as much as I have researching and writing it. Apart from the revelations of my Dad's memoirs, finding out more about the ship SS Fairsky, our sea voyage passed many different countries, a Suez Canal transit and Aden's drama; the many Ten Pound Poms and their stories and the extreme environment and isolation of Port Hedland in the early sixties; it has been great fun and strangely cathartic exploring my own perceptions and perspectives of the time.

I have laughed and cried upon rediscovering a place and a time that had become as remote to me as the rest of the world seemed, when we first arrived in Port Hedland some fifty years ago; a tiny town miles from anywhere that was to shape our lives and future in ways we could not have imagined then.

I've been asked many times if I will go back to Port Hedland and the answer is yes; but not back—the "back" is contained within the pages of this book— the future always invites us to create a new, different adventure.

Stephen Outram
Author of *The First Five Years*.

A New Life

Southampton 1964

> "My mother cried, in sixty five
> when we left those British Isles
> We all held hands, there were no brass bands
> as we faced twelve thousand miles"

It was with both apprehension and excitement that we climbed SS Fairsky's gangplank on Boxing Day 1964. A bleak, grey sky was snowing down on us and our loved ones: Mum and Pop Outram, my sister Patricia, her husband Peter and their two boys, with whom we'd spent Christmas Day, watched sadly from the jetty. They seemed to have grown smaller as I looked back to wave just before stepping through the gangway and onboard. It was a cold and windy day at the Port of Southampton, and the big ship strained against its mooring ropes as if restless and eager to get going.

I'm looking up at the long gangplank that seems to go on forever and following my Dad; he knows where to go. As we near the top, I'm sure that I can see a brightly coloured parrot perched on the ship's rail, peering down at me. I look for my Dad to tell him about the bird but he has gone. And then I see his hand reach out and run to grab it as he lifts me up high and hauls me onto the ship, and into my future.

There was a rush to find our cabin and off-load luggage so that we could get back up on deck; the tugs were taking their positions ready to coax the twelve thousand five hundred ton, five hundred foot ship away from the docks. We just made it topside in time as the gangplanks were being removed, and the thousands of streaming paper tapes that linked us with the land began to break away. Crowding the rail with the other passengers we all waved blindly into the sea of upturned faces below us, not really sure where the family was but hoping they could see us.

A thin strip of water appeared between our ship and the docks and grew wider and wider. Southampton gradually faded behind a thickening blanket of drifting snow flakes that echoed a final, long blast from the foghorn back to us. Soon enough, Fairsky was nosing out into the English Channel carrying Trevor, Molly, Stephen and Karen away from England and on to a new world, and a new life.

We were bound for Australia!

Why?

Immigrate? To Australia?

Why would two English people with young children—
one starting school—good jobs and a supportive family
travel twelve thousand miles away to live in Australia?
That's the question my father, Reginald Edward
Outram, had asked me, with some anger, when I told
him about my plans to immigrate. My mother, Dorothy
May, sat in tears and wouldn't look at me.

I was thirty one years old and my father was still able
to make me nervous when he spoke that way. I had
explained about the job opportunities, much better
wages and the chance to build a better life in a new
country. He had shaken his head and looked away; he
didn't understand; perhaps he didn't want to understand.
Mother had left and gone to her bedroom.

In the early sixties, Molly and I lived with our two
young children, Karen and Stephen, in a small caravan
in the village of Brandon, Suffolk. I was working as an
aircraft engineer earning eleven pounds a week and
Molly did part-time hairdressing, though, was mostly
busy with the children. We had little money, no car
and our life in England was typical middle-lower class.
Stephen had begun school and I could see his life
beginning much the same as mine had, and my life was
following a similar pattern to my father's; I was hungry

17

for more. The idea of Australia had really excited me and while Molly was relatively happy living in England, she was willing to go. She'd told me that she didn't want me to say to her, later in life, that she'd held me back.

We'd already made the application, twice; the first one had been lost by the immigration people and we'd had to go through the whole process again. Now we had been approved, paid the fees and were getting ready to go. This caused a great deal of difficulty for my father and, at one point, he became quite bitter. He told me that if I did this thing, this foolish trip to Australia, he would no longer consider me his son. Both of my parents were deeply disappointed that I was breaking up the family and taking their two grandchildren away; especially Stephen who was the family name bearer. It was with a heavy heart, but also a new found determination to succeed, that I left their Seven Oaks home for the last time.

Molly was an only child and her parents, George and Rena Edwards, were not very happy with me either. George was a tradesman; a Master Painter and a club man who liked his beer, and I copped the nasty side of his tongue one evening. It was hard for both of our relatives to accept that we were going, but I knew this was right for us and I was going to make it work.

We visited with Molly's parents in Bradford, to say goodbye, and then went to my sister's home; Patricia lived at Portsmouth. All of my family would be there for Christmas Day, 1964. Her bungalow was a short distance from Southampton, where we would be leaving from, and they would drive us to the docks on Boxing Day. It was a last chance to see everyone and, hopefully, make some peace.

My Dad has made, by hand, a beautiful model steam ship; it's a Christmas present for Grandad Outram. It has big wooden wheels on either side, a red funnel and a green hull. I watched him put it together; all of the tiny pieces. My Dad is really clever. We are at Aunty Patricia and Uncle Peter's house in their lounge room with the fire crackling, and it's time for presents.

Granddad Outram is unwrapping his present and lifting away tissue paper; the model ship comes out of its box. My Dad is there with him. A mast is broken and Dad says he will fix it; the model must have been bumped when we packed. Grandad puts the ship on top of the coffee table in front of him and turns away to talk to Uncle Peter; he hasn't smiled once. Did he like his present?

My Dad carefully picks up the model and takes it into the dining room, to repair the mast at the table. He comes back later leaving the ship in the other room. It's a funny Christmas.

Stephen Outram

The First 12,000 Miles

Bound for Australia

"And my Dad stood tall and told us all
of the seeds that we would sow
When we set sail for Australia
All those years ago"

Crossing the English Channel was uneventful and
the small islands of Guernsey and Jersey passed by
unnoticed; we were busy unpacking and organising our
cabins and exploring the ship. The children shared one
small cabin and Molly and I had another containing
two single bunk beds, a wardrobe and basin; there was a
bathroom down the corridor. Both cabins were internal,
so no porthole and instead, a ceiling vent puffed fresh
air into the room. There were around one thousand
adults and five hundred children on board, all to be
let off at various ports around Australia; our port was
Fremantle in Western Australia.

The Bay of Biscay, which can be very rough due to
its relatively shallow waters, was not kind to us and
everyone except Molly suffered sea sickness; she became
our nurse. We went to the dining room for the evening
meal but were unable to eat; most of the long lines
of tables were empty and we returned to our cabins.
During the night Fairsky turned left at Portugal, slipped
passed Gibraltar and squeezed through its famous strait,

where the water was calmer and we began to get our sea legs and feel better. With Spain now on our port side the Alboran Sea opened up before us and after a time, seemlessly transformed into the great "middle sea;" the Mediterranean Sea. The ship sailed on past Majorca and Sardinia, making good way, and the rumbling of her great engines was becoming more and more familiar, and strangely comforting. The Sicilian town of Masala, perched on the foot of Italy, winked at us as Fairsky swung away towards the southeast where Malta eventually appeared on our starboard side.

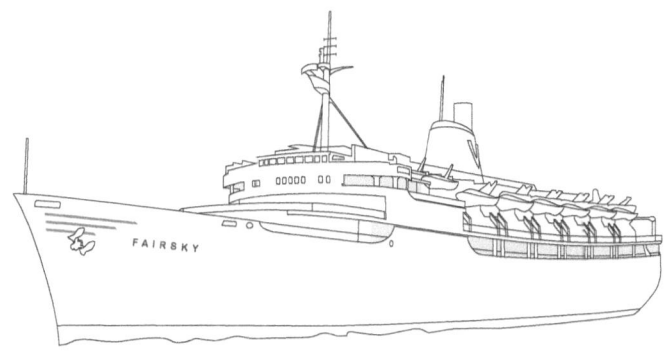

SS Fairsky, of the Sitmar Line

I had been watching for Malta, and seeing the city of Valetta and The Grand Harbour brought back fond memories. All of us, except for Karen who was born in Cambridge, had been here before. During my service with the Royal Navy, I was stationed in Malta for two years; Molly had gone with me and in August 1956 our first child, Stephen, was born in the Royal Navy Hospital, Mtarfa.

I had managed to join the navy at sixteen years old. Being underage, one of my parents had to sign the application form, giving their permission. My mother, Dorothy, agreed provided that I write her a letter every week that I was away. I kept my promise and did this faithfully, every week, until the day she died some fifty six years later.

Malta was quite hot and Molly, young Stephen and I would often go swimming in the sea. We would take bottles of Coca Cola, swim out and drop them into the clear waters; later I'd dive down to retrieve them from the sandy bottom where they had cooled down ready for drinking. Happy memories of another time; another adventure.

Oh ... that cool water feels so good. I'm splashing, laughing! What's that touching me? A jelly fish? Ouch! It's all right, Mum's got me.

Our immigration to Australia had been sponsored by Tony Wiles, who was a friend from my naval days. His father, Keith, had a taxi business in the town of Port Hedland, which was located one thousand two hundred miles north of Fremantle. A taxi driver job was on offer if I wanted it, paying twenty five pounds a week. As an aircraft engineer working in England I had been earning eleven pounds, so this seemed too good to refuse!

I had two other jobs to look into: one was working for Qantas Airways in Sydney, New South Wales; and the second with the Australian Government in Melbourne, Victoria making the French Mirage Interceptor aircraft, which had been selected to replace the fifteen year old Sabre fighter. Three good options, albeit in different corners of a very large continent.

Our fare to Australia was just twenty pounds; ten pounds for each adult and the children travelled free. The rules were that we had to stay for two years and our sponsor, Tony, was responsible for us. After two years in Australia we were free to go home to England, paying our own fares. And so we found ourselves onboard SS Fairsky, cruising the Mediterranean and on our way to the other side of the planet.

We had just one chance to go ashore on our twelve thousand mile sea voyage, Aden[1], but first we had to travel Egypt's famous Suez Canal.

Sitting in the most southeasterly part of the Mediterranean Sea, at the tip of the African Continent, is Port Said, guarding the entrance to a one hundred and fifteen mile long, man-made canal, which feeds out into the Red Sea on the other side. Fairsky dropped anchor outside of Port Said to queue before entering the Suez Canal. We went up on deck and watched as a plethora of small boats approached the ship and the locals began to ply their trade. The boats were a small, strongly made wooden craft; rowboats that were packed with goods for sale. Brown skinned faces capped with cotton caps looked up at us and their white teeth flashed as these Egyptian retailers called up to us. Their ropes were fastened to the ship's rail and used to pull reed baskets, full of goods, up to the passengers, who were peering down into the boats at the various items on offer.

There was lots of shouting, nodding and pointing as

---

1   Aden became the capital city of South Yemen in 1967, when the British had left.

traders and passengers tried to communicate. The idea was that you took an item from the basket and replaced it with some money. The traders would then haul the basket down to inspect your offering and either accept it or send the basket back for more. It was confusing, strange and quite a lot of fun. I had no idea what the traders were calling out, but somehow we ended up with some items and everyone seemed happy.

Yay! Karen and I got some toys. I have a camel and she has a sheep. They came up in baskets from the boat people. Dad gave me some money to put in the basket and they pulled that basket down really fast. I don't know what they are calling out but they seem pretty excited. Some people are throwing coins down into the water and boys, the boat people, are diving in to get them. I am going to learn to swim like a fish so I can do that and get some coins too.

Eventually Fairsky's horn sounded; its giant anchor chain rattled, shaking off a million water droplets, and we began moving; it was time to enter the Suez Canal. The ship slowly picked up speed and I watched the shoreline narrow to become two parallel lines. The buildings and busyness of Port Said gradually gave way to villages and then sand dunes as we moved deeper into the canal.

We all went up to the top deck and as we sailed slowly by, it was quite hypnotising watching mile after mile of undulating sand dunes. We were occasionally relieved by tall palm trees and nomadic people on their camels. The children were soon bored and went off to play. After a time the canal opened up into Timsah Lake and Ismailia—the city of beauty and enchantment—

came into view off our starboard side. It was a welcome diversion and our eyes fed hungrily on its clusters of green trees and regular geometry, in sharp contrast to the bright sand that had been our view. Ismailia moved in behind us and unable to keep up with Fairsky, faded into the distance.

We were over half way through the canal now and soon its straight, regular lines gave way to the more shapely Great Bitter Lakes. Before the Suez Canal was built, this area was a large, dry salt valley, which may give some clue as to its name. The lake narrowed down again to once again become the familiar, parallel, sand-lined banks dotted with sparse, scrubby vegetation.

Then, after leaving the Mediterranean some fifteen hours earlier, Egypt's northeasterly seaport of Suez came into view and the ancient Red Sea opened up wide before us. Fortunately, Moses and his people had passed this way many hundreds of years before and we sailed on without intervention. The Red Sea narrowed and channeled us into the Arabian Sea, where Fairsky was scheduled to dock in Aden at "Steamer Port," known as Tawahi.

We had only one day in Aden and wanted to do some duty free shopping. We were advised to get a taxi to "The Crater," and were told it was a poorer district but had plenty of shops. Crater (or Kraytar), Aden's ancient port city, is situated in the crater of a dormant volcano, which forms the Shamsan Mountains.

The thirty minute taxi ride took us about five miles across Aden and we were dropped off in a drab but busy street. Alighting from the taxi we were immediately surrounded by beggars; they were all children, mostly cripples, no hands, one arm, one leg and their fingers and faces were stained with the distinctive mark of the Betel Nut, which they chewed. The nut is known for inducing mild euphoria and feelings of wellbeing; which may have been comforting to these very poor people.

I'm anxious and stay close to Dad. They have crowded in so close that I can smell their strange breath and see the flies clinging to their eyes. They are children; my age and younger with dark skin that is stained red around their mouths. I can see that some have no hands or arms; my nervousness changes to sadness and I wonder what their life must be like in these hot, dirty streets with no feet to kick a football or fingers to catch one with.

Dad suddenly pushes through the crowd and I put my head down and follow him and Mum, watching our feet puff up the dust that settles on our English leather shoes and the many bare brown feet.

We had to be strong and push past the beggars; it was very sad to see. I broke through them and gathered my family with me as we quickly moved on to explore the area. We found plenty of shops and I bought a tape recorder and radios for the children, a sewing machine for Molly, and a blender. I also got a 35mm film camera with leather strap and case, which was to serve us well in the years to come.

I am so excited! A new transistor radio. Batteries, solid state, chrome tuning knob, a pull out aerial and a leather case. I can't wait to get back to the boat to try it out. Come on you lot, let's go!

We had a lot to carry and really needed some help. As if by magic a tall, thin Arab man adopted us to become our porter and local guide. It was hot and dry and we were all parched, I bought some chilled bottles of Coca Cola from a street vendor, which did the trick nicely.

I'm thirsty and want to drink the whole bottle down in one go! Dad says, "No, son." as he does, and gives me a straw that's wrapped in thin, clear plastic. I rip it open, put the paper straw in my bottle and suck. My ears are buzzing and my cheeks pull in as I try to get as much of the cold Coke into my mouth as possible. I can feel the bubbles racing down my throat; they reach my stomach and then bounce back up again. I do a big burp and Mum says, "Stephen!" as she does. Dad says that we have to use straws because there may be germs on the bottle.

I finish my drink quickly and would like another one but we are off walking again. Oh well. There are no rubbish bins and I drop the empty bottle in the dirty gutter. Glancing back I see a boy picking it up; he tips the bottle up and shakes the last few drops into his mouth. For a brief second our eyes meet and then he turns away, taking the bottle with him.

Molly wanted some gold earrings and our new guide picked up the boxes and bags, then lead us down narrow back streets and alleys to a goldsmith; we had no idea where we were. We kept the children close and were frightened, and worried, wondering if we would ever see the ship again!

While we were in a shop negotiating on some jewelry, Molly noticed that Karen was missing. She looked around the jumble of shelves and boxes, then went outside into the street and found our guide with the little girl. Molly shouted angrily at him, rushed over and grabbed Karen's hand, pulling her back into the shop with us; it was a tense moment. We were done with the Crater and our guide took us back to where we had started from and found us a taxi. Not knowing what to pay, I gave him a pound. He smiled, we shook hands and I thanked him; glad to be safe and very glad to be heading back to the ship and getting aboard again! I think we had someone looking after us on that day.

I read some time later that in 1967, just two years after our visit, there was an event known as the Aden Emergency, which was an insurgency against the British Crown forces by rival Arab nationals. It actually began in 1963, with the throwing of a grenade at a gathering of British officials at Aden Airport, and escalated in 1967.

> "... a British infantry battalion marched into the *Crater* with a pipe-band playing traditional regimental tunes, and managed to occupy the whole district ..."—Wikipedia

In November 1967, British forces withdrew and the independent People's Republic of South Yemen was proclaimed, with Aden as its capital. Perhaps, while in the Crater, Molly and I were picking up on the unrest that was telling us to take very good care while we were in a troubled area.

With all of the passengers safely back on board, Fairsky sailed out of Steamer Point, turned west into the Gulf of Aden and then we were off; our next stop Fremantle in Australia. I think they had the accelerator flat to the boards, as every rivet in the ship seemed to be shaking.

Full steam ahead to Australia!

The Great Ocean

Seven Thousand to Go

The Arabian Sea spills out into the Gulf of Aden, which then becomes the great Indian Ocean. On the other side of this massive body of water, over six thousand eight hundred miles away, was Australia. We would not set foot on land again for some fifteen days. Fairsky steamed past the small island of Socotra as we gathered at the ship's stern to watch the great landmasses of Africa and Asia sink slowly into the sea. We joked about going faster when the ship reached the equator and begun to sail *down* the curvature of the planet, to the antipodes. Fairsky's bow was pointed east towards Sri Lanka at the tip of India, where we would turn south to cross the equator, so we would find out in several days.

Life on board fell into a routine that was punctuated with breakfast, lunch and dinner; we often ate in the forward dining room and made friends with a couple who also had two small children. Susanna and Peter were going to Western Australia too. She had worked as a dancer; a Tiller Girl[1] at the London Palladium, and

---

1   The Tiller Girls, first formed by John Tiller, were among the most popular dance troupes of the 1900s. Possibly most famous for their high-kicking routines; they were highly trained and precise; the girls all of similar height and stature.

Peter was a musician who had played in a London band. They were hoping to get similar work in Perth and we agreed to keep in touch after we'd landed.

It was very pleasant to swim in the pool, sit in the sun and not have to work, cook or wash up. We relaxed into life onboard and enjoyed a variety of entertainment, particularly the evening's dinner dances. The children were well taken care of with their own playroom, a good library and organised activities.

During the day, Stephen could always be found in the pool and Karen enjoyed it too. The crew drained one of the main pools and brought the water level down to about two feet deep, for the younger children. Stephen couldn't swim yet and used a float tube. One day Molly and I were sunning on deck chairs, reading our books, when he came running up, dripping wet and very excited.

I love the pool. It has salt water from the ocean. It's a long way climbing down the ladder to get into the water. They let all the water out for the children's swim-time. I'm carrying a rubber ring down with me. I suppose I could just throw it in from the top but I'd probably hit someone and get into trouble. I can see one of the crew down there; a life guard.

I can't swim yet. When the sea is rough, like today, the waves in the pool swish around from side to side; it's fun. I'm down and jump off the ladder into the water. Splash! I wonder if I can swim by myself today?

I'm kicking around in the tube and let my body slide out, with just my fingertips holding on. Suddenly a wave grabs my tube and pushes it away; my fingers

31

slip off and for a second I float, my face down in the water. Then my arms move and my legs kick again and I realise that I'm swimming; a jerky kind of breaststroke that I've seen Mum and Dad do. I'm swimming!

I swim from one side of the pool to the other and then back again, up and down with the waves, then across to the ladder where I hold on for a while. My heart is pounding with excitement. Brilliant! No more tubes. I can swim. Did Mum and Dad see me? Hey, I can swim!

Molly wrapped a towel around him as he told us, very proudly, that he had swum without the tube. No one had taught him; he had managed it by himself. We were delighted with the news. Both of us were keen swimmers; I had competed, representing the navy in water polo and diving, and Molly was a local champion in Bradford, where she grew up; we both knew what it was like to take those first strokes unaided. Stephen, who could never sit still for long, ran off to swim some more. We didn't see him again until dinner.

Passengers were encouraged by the crew to form sporting groups and organise on-deck events. We tried our hand at deck quoits and I played some table tennis, we also enjoyed a variety of card games. We read a lot, talked with other passengers, walked the decks and swam for exercise. After a while it became a task to entertain myself and I longed for the ship to reach Australia so that we could get on with the next leg of our trip. Karen, who was five years old, seemed quite contented and played happily or slept.

We had now passed Sri Lanka, turned south and were in the Indian Ocean when notices began to go up about a special equator crossing ceremony, featuring the great Sea God Neptune. It was a welcome diversion and we chatted with our excited children about what might be presented.

"Grand Equatorial Ceremony
Hear Ye! Hear Ye!

All loyal subjects of His most Serene Majesty King Neptune are requested to come to the Sun Deck at 4.p.m [sic] and bow in submission to their Liege Lord."—Printed Program, Fairsky, 1965

On January 12, 1965 we all gathered on deck for the equatorial crossing and our appointed meeting with Neptune. We noticed absolutely no difference in the ship's speed as 4:00 p.m. passed by and Fairsky began her downhill run, in fact, nothing much changed at all.

King Neptune arrived adorned with an impressive, albeit slightly dented, bejewelled crown that sparkled in the afternoon sun. Mock seaweed hair tumbled down past his shoulders to compliment his long flowing sea-green robes. He was accompanied by his wife, who was lead by a Sea Horse person and an entourage of other dubious deep sea creatures and tattooed Polynesian warriors. Following their parade along the deck, festivities began. The crew enticed various passengers to participate in a series of entertaining skits and the whole thing was boisterous, loud and great fun. We lifted the children up so they could see over the crowd; Stephen was on my shoulders and Molly held Karen.

Someone is on the operating table with a big white sheet pulled over them. King Neptune is there too, looking on. I can only see their head poking out. The sea doctor has a knife and is doing something under the sheet. Oh gosh! A big pile of intestines just got pulled out (I didn't know they looked like sausages). And now he's pulling out more and dropping them into a bucket; and still more. That's a lot. Hope we don't get them for dinner. The doctor is getting something out of his black bag. A huge thermometer! Wow! Glad I'm not sick and getting that in my mouth. Put me down Dad, I've got to get a closer look.

After a lot of fun on deck we went back to our cabin to get ready for dinner; a special menu had been prepared for the event. Seated amongst an excited group of diners, we had the choice of consommè, chicken cream soup with profiteroles or ravioli for entrée; the main course was lobster with Russian salad or roast giant turkey, tropical style with cranberry sauce—there was also a huge cold buffet—and for desert, apple pancake or caramel potatoes. And everyone received an elaborate 'Crossing the Line' printed certificate[2] to take with them and mark the historic occasion.

Eleven days later we sailed slowly past Western Australia's Rottnest Island and on into the Port of Fremantle.

---

2   In 2014, while writing this book, I noticed several of the equatorial crossing certificates being offered on eBay; forty nine year old vintage collectables.

34

Fremantle 102

Welcome to Australia

"A month at sea feeling strange but free
then Rottnest slid slowly by
We set down in Fremantle
'neath a cloudless summer sky"

Around seven thousand years ago, sea levels rose closing a natural land bridge that connected the elevated, limestone landscape of Rottnest Island to Tera Australis, "South Land." This isolated a chain of three islands some twelve miles offshore. Garden, Carnac and Rottnest Islands were left sitting amongst ancient coral reefs, washed by the warm Leeuwin Current that flows southwards down the Western Australian coastline.

The morning of January 22, 1965 was dead calm, hardly a breeze ruffled the smooth surface. Fairsky's bow pushed out giant ripples that would caress Rottnest's white sand shores long after we had passed. The decks were crowded with passengers greedily feasting on the first land they had seen for weeks and looking on to the vast mainland, low and blue in the distance. It was hot; very hot and the sun cut through our hair and ripped at our delicate English scalps.

Ninety minutes later and twenty eight days after leaving England we sailed into the Port of Fremantle, and into a one hundred degree heat wave[1]. Two muscular tug boats came out to greet us and gently nudged the big white ship up against the docks. Fairsky took-on the mooring ropes without fuss, happy to come to rest after the long voyage.

There were no streaming paper tapes this time and no welcoming family to wave at. We were packed and dressed, and waited impatiently, though somewhat medicated by the intense heat. Finally the gangplanks were fitted, the gangways opened and passengers jostled each other in their hurry to disembark. I bid Fairsky, goodbye and at the same time said hello to Australia; I'm sure I heard a low chuckle as the sweat ran off my brow, down my cheek and disappeared into the collar of my shirt.

I left the ship as I had entered it, wearing a suit and tie with an overcoat draped over my arm; Molly had on pants, long-sleeved top, a scarf and jacket; and the children were dressed in shorts, shirts and a jumper. We wanted to look good coming into Australia and were to suffer our heavy English fabrics and overdress.

The big yellow and blue building is next to the ship. We are up high and I can see into the building; the side is all glass. There are a lot of people inside and Dad says that's where we have to go to get into Australia. There are no boat people around the ship

---

1   "Perth residents are expected to experience the city's hottest consecutive number of days of high temperatures since 1965, with the mercury forecast to hover around 40 degrees for the next seven days and peaking on Saturday with a 42C scorcher."— Samantha Leung, PerthNow, 2012

this time. Our soft camel and sheep that we got in
Aden were taken away by a man. Mum said that
they couldn't get into Australia because they were
probably stuffed with old hospital bandages. They
seemed all right to me. Karen cried.

It's hot. I'm taking my jumper off but Mum says
to leave it because we have to look good for the
customs man. She says he's a very important man.
The gangplank is down and we're getting off with all
the other people.

Stepping off the gangplank and on to Victoria Quay,
Molly and I held the children's hands as we followed
the crowd that moved haltingly towards the Port of
Fremantle Passenger Terminal; someone said it was the
largest building of its kind in Australia. Its exterior was
brightly decorated with an ochre, blue and cream colour
scheme, and a wide awning beckoned us, providing
welcome relief from the sun when we finally reached it.

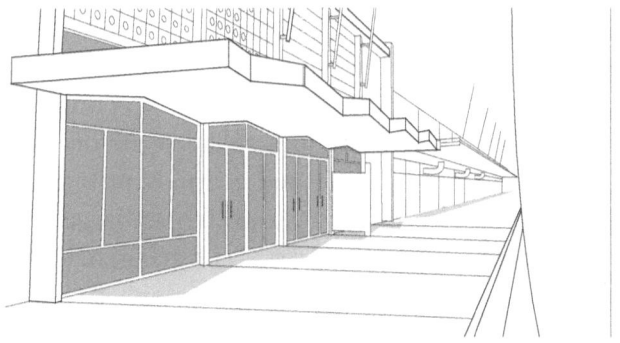

Passenger Terminal

The terminal opened up inside to its full two story

height, flanked by full-wall glass panels that looked out over the ships, and reached up to frame the ceiling high above us. The hall was full of people; excited, talking, looking, pointing, laughing, shuffling and noisy.

It's taken ages to get into the building. There are people everywhere. It's big in here and very noisy. Mum is holding my hand and Karen's too; Dad is in front. Up ahead I can see a big sign that reads, Customs Hall. That must be where the very important customs man lives. I wonder why he's so important? I might be able to get my jumper off soon.

As we approached the custom's barrier an official greeted us. His light blue shirt was soaking wet and Terry Jones, Australian Customs was written on his name tag. I asked him if Fremantle was normally as hot as this. Terry grinned and told me that for this time of year it was, and the temperature is 102! With that, he officially welcomed us to Australia. Our paper work was inspected and stamped; he counted heads, said hello to the children and then waved us on through.

The baggage collection area was next and we gathered our suitcases. The rest of our gear, our worldly goods and chattels packed in wooden chests, had come over in Fairsky's hold; these would be stored in Fremantle until we called for them. We moved on to walk past large banks of escalators, shops, native art, car hire agencies, banks, florists, cafes and the like—the business of travel was alive and well.

Well, the very important customs man didn't have to wear a jumper! He was all sweaty; his shirt was all wet. We're through now and he can't see me anymore.

I'm taking my jumper off. Phew, that's better. Mum says I have to carry it until we get outside. Are we there yet?

Often, through the rumble of voices we heard snatches of conversation—the Australian accent with its unmistakable "twang" jingled in our ears and we all laughed. Molly and I looked at each other then down to the children, their eyes were bright and it all felt good. Soon we found ourselves outside in the sun again, standing on the departures concourse. We were in Australia with our feet on firm ground, which felt very strange after four weeks on the ship.

I had been exchanging letters with our sponsor, Tony Wiles, for some months from England and we'd arranged that he would pick us up at the terminal. I left the children with Molly and walked around the pickup area but could not see him, so we waited. There were people everywhere, some being collected by friends, others hailing taxis or getting on busses. We waited. The busses came and went as did the taxis, cars and people. We waited. After several hours Molly was annoyed, the children bored and fidgety and I was beginning to realise that Tony was not coming. The day was moving on, we had not booked any accommodation and we were all hungry and travel weary.

Again, I left Molly with the children and our pile of suitcases, and went off to locate someone who could help us. I saw a sign that read, Migrant Information Services. The uniformed official at the counter was obviously used to dealing with homeless, lost migrants and quickly directed me to a waiting bus, which would take us to a hostel accommodating newly arrived migrants. I was very relieved and rushed back to tell the others. We picked up our bags and ran, glad to be moving again.

While the driver stored our luggage, we climbed aboard and found seats towards the back. When the bus was full he swung the door shut, ground his gears and we moved off with a jerk. Every window was wide open and some people had put their heads or arms outside, while others unconsciously leaned towards the small openings savoring the breeze.

We left Fremantle and were soon speeding along the Stirling Highway, headed into Western Australia's capital city, Perth and Graylands[2].

---

2   The suburb Graylands was renamed to Mount Claremont in 1988.

Plan B

Perth and the Irishman

Graylands Migrant Hostel, characterised by its Nissan
huts made from a half-cylindrical skin of corrugated
steel, operated from 1956 - 1981. It was a former
military base that had been re-purposed by the
Government to house migrants, like us, who had been
encouraged to make Australia their home. Our bus
turned off Alfred Road, drove through the front gate
along a driveway and halted in a cloud of dust near
an administration building. We got out, collected our
suitcases, were duly processed and then directed to our
accommodation. Silver City, as it was affectionately
known, was to be our home for the next week or so.

The hostel was a staging post for migrants who,
generally, moved out when they found work and took
up other accommodation. Later, we discovered that
several families were sitting out their two years in the
hostel, saying that the Immigration Service hadn't given
them jobs and houses; they thought that everything was
going to be handed to them on a plate!

The charge for each family was twelve pounds per week
with the first week being free. The huts were old but
clean and fairly spacious; there was a door at each end
and small bay windows dotted along the length. Food
was provided and served, cafeteria-style, in another

41

building. The public showers and toilets were functional and similar to a caravan park, except that the children were nervous to go inside them because of the large spiders and other strange looking insects that they'd not seen before.

Nissan huts at Graylands Migrant Hostel

Except for the resident wildlife, we thought it was great! We could stroll to the Swan River and swim and play with the children upon white sand beaches and under blue skies. King's Park and the Botanical Gardens were also within walking distance. The park was elevated and we could see the Swan River, like a great silver snake below us, and look out at Perth's sprawling skyline.

Our sponsor, Tony Wiles, eventually found us. He had been out playing a country cricket week in Perth and had picked up a new taxi. Tony was going to drive the twelve hundred miles back to Port Hedland after the cricket was finished. It was really good to see a familiar face; I shook his hand warmly and introduced him to Molly and the children.

Over the next few days, in between his cricket matches, Tony drove us around to see more of Kings Park and some of Perth's beaches—Scarborough and Cottesloe. We all caught a bus into Perth for the day and found London Court, a British styled shopping arcade; it seemed very familiar and for a moment we imagined that we were back in England! He took us out one night for a meal near the Swan River, which was lovely with the city's lights dancing across its surface. We ate near the Narrows Bridge where there was a huge illuminated windmill with lights sprayed across its outstretched sails. And we saw Perth's famous Swan Brewery, which featured the outline of a large swan that could be seen for miles. Perth at night, from Kings Park and along the river, was an absolute delight. Fun times.

There was a niggling question in our minds that wouldn't let go and Molly and I talked about it. It went something like this,

> If we didn't like Australia, or this trip didn't work out for us, then where would we obtain the money to return to England at the end of our two year term?

A few days later, by design or good fortune, a well dressed Irishman came to Silver City selling real estate—three acre plots of undeveloped land, located eighteen miles out of Perth, for five hundred and seventy five pounds each. Prior to leaving England we had sold our caravan home for five hundred pounds; it made up most of the money we had. I decided to have a look at the land, thinking that it could become our ticket home if necessary.

The following morning the Irishman bundled all of us into his car, and we drove out of Perth into the bush.

After a while, he pulled off the bitumen road and took us down a bumpy one-lane dirt track, bordered by tall grass and bush either side. It opened up where several tracks crossed and he pulled up right on the intersection in a cloud of billowing red dust.

He glanced outside and told us that this was it. We looked around at the dense scrub with its tall gum trees and grasses, looked at each other in some confusion, and asked him where was what. He laughed and explained that the land was soon to be cleared and that we were getting in early, the very best time to buy. He pointed to some white surveyor's stakes tied with red tape. We all got out.

The road is just dirt; it's red-brown dirt. And the forest is really thick. Are we going to live here? Where will our caravan go? Big tall trees with white bark and all of their leaves bunched at the top. I can hear a really loud buzzing sound. Lots of insects, I guess? Perhaps there's mosquitoes and those big Australian spiders. Whoa! I wonder if they have snakes around here? I reach out and touch the tall grass at the edge of the track; it's strong, wide and, ouch, sharp! I can't really see the plot they are all talking about, but this place seems really alive. I like it. That Irishman talks a lot but he sounds good, like a song. Dad is shaking hands with him. Mum is smiling. Karen stayed in the car, she's looking out of the window. She sees me and waves.

The plot was long and narrow with the short boundary fronted by the dirt track. Our soft talking Irishman assured us that there would be proper roads built soon enough.

Next to it were other similar plots; seven in all. I decided to buy it and struck a deal with the Irishman; one hundred pounds down and repayments of five pounds per week for two years. At the end of the term, it would be fully paid for and hopefully, would provide the money to return to England if we needed to sell it.

We climbed into his car again, to drive back to Perth and sign some papers. This was good and I felt like we had taken some positive steps. This was the first plot of land we had ever bought; just a few days in Australia and we were land owners. It would have taken us years of work, scrimping and saving to do that in England. I was beginning to really like this place!

Tony had already left to drive back to Port Hedland and we decided that we had better get on with our lives and made arrangements to travel by aeroplane. I contacted the storage company and they would send our chests to Tony's place by truck. And so, ten days after arriving in Perth we flew out at six in the morning. It was Monday, February 1, 1965, our flight was in a Douglas DC-3 airliner and the first stop on the way was Geraldton, wherever that was!

More Flies Than People

The Milk Run

"And the plane up to Port Hedland
was hot and cramped and slow
As we wiped the flies, from our eyes
All those years ago"

The Douglas DC-3 was a fixed-wing, propeller-driven airliner that revolutionized air transport in the 1930s; I had worked on the Dakota in England. It carried over 20 passengers and could cruise at one hundred and eighty knots. It was a good aircraft and widely used in Europe and America. Our flight had the word Ansett stencilled proudly on its fuselage.

With a roar and a lurch we lifted off from Perth Airport and got a chance to see some of the city from the air, as the plane banked before levelling out and heading north. Even at six in the morning the heat on the ground was intense. The aircraft gained height and as the drone of its Pratt & Whitney Twin Wasp engines eased, we cooled off in the air conditioning and relaxed back in our seats.

We were on the milk run, which meant stopping at every town on the way to deliver mail and goods. The trip to Port Hedland included stops at Geraldton, Carnarvon, Onslow and Roebourne. Geraldton was about two hundred and thirty miles away.

We were only in the air for about an hour or so when the pitch of the engines changed slightly and the aircraft began to descend. Twenty minutes later, we bumped onto the runway and were pushed forward against our seat belts amidst the roar of two powerful engines revving in reverse thrust. Our DC-3 swung neatly into a parking bay and came to a halt; we were told we could get off for fifteen minutes. There were two things I noticed while climbing down the narrow, metal steps to reach the ground: it was hotter and there were a lot more flies.

Geraldton Airport had been home to a RAAF Flying Training School and then been redeveloped in 1958 for civil use; the runway was tarmac and there was a terminal building into which the pilot had disappeared. Several new passengers strolled over and hung around outside until the pilot returned, and then everyone climbed onboard and we were off again.

This was repeated three more times as we progressed further north, up the Western Australian coastline. Most of the airports had graded, dirt runways and often just a tin shed. With each stop the temperature got hotter and there were more flies.

I'm getting off the plane and my eyes are squinting tight against the bright sun. It is so hot. I feel weak. We are on flat red dirt and next to the plane there's a small shed. It's like a bus shelter built with old tree branches and it has a wrinkled tin roof. I go over and sit on the seat. I burn my bare legs and sit on the edge. I'm sweating.

There are lots of small, black flies. Sticky, annoying flies. They are in my eyes, my ears and up my nose. It's time to go again. I must have a million flies on my shoulders and back. Mum brushes them away but they come back really fast.

It grew hotter and hotter as we went on and gradually, we stripped the children of their clothing. Each time the doors of the aircraft opened more flies got on and hitched a free ride north. There seemed to be more flies than people. Looking around at the empty seats it seemed that Port Hedland was of more interest to the insects than it was to anyone else.

We touched down, for the last time, in the afternoon and were greeted by Port Hedland airport's very simple terminal building and a host of flies (I guess they were there to pick up all the ones that were travelling on our flight). I gathered the children and Molly together, and we picked up our luggage in the terminal and headed for the exit. Just outside there was a dusty, white car with a Port Hedland Taxis sign on it, and a familiar face grinned at us from behind the windshield.

Our travelling was done for now; we had made it to our new home in Australia. As Tony drove us into town along Wilson Street, Molly and I looked around at the unremarkable sparse landscape and wondered what we had gotten ourselves into.

Sleeping Giant

Port Hedland, 1965

Port Hedland is situated one thousand two hundred miles north of Perth, high up on the Western Australian coastline. The town is tucked-in behind a large sand dune known as Finucane Island, which created a natural, sheltered harbour about three quarters of a mile across. Immediately southwest of the town site and shaped like a great hand[1] was Stingray Creek, with its four long fingers pointing inland. With tides in the area reaching highs of twenty five feet, the creek flows out into the harbour and rushes past Finucan at an impressive rate of knots, on the ebb tide.

It's not widely known that Port Headland is an island that was regularly cut off from the mainland by tides that crept inland through low lying tidal-flats and tropical Mangrove forests. In the late 1800s the 7 Mile Causeway was built of sandstone rocks supporting a bitumen topped road. This opened the way for local pastoral activities to access the port. Wool bales and other produce were transported by camel, drovers brought their cattle and put them in holding yards near a large Tamarind tree, and all were shipped out via a

---

1   The traditional owners are the Karriyarra people; their name for the area is "Marapikurrinya," which may refer to the hand-shaped formation of tidal creeks that extend the harbour.

newly constructed timber jetty.

In 1890 alluvial gold was discovered nearby, and the town of Marble Bar was gazetted the next year to support the mining. A one hundred and fourteen mile narrow-gauge railway line was opened in 1912, bringing gold and tin ore into Port Hedland. The airport was built in 1920 and at the same time a fleet of five pearling luggers set up business in the port, based in a hut on Finucane Island.

The rail link survived until 1950 and then Port Hedland dozed for ten years until a twenty year old Government embargo[2], preventing the export of iron ore, was lifted and six million tons of iron ore known as Mount Goldsworthy became viable. A consortium of three mining companies formed Mount Goldsworthy Mining Associates in 1963 and was granted an export licence. Port Hedland, only eighty miles away and the obvious choice for a port, began to awaken from its slumber.

When we arrived, the population was twelve hundred people. In town there were two main pubs—the Pier Hotel and the Esplanade Hotel; one general store, which sold everything and doubled as the Post Office; one garage, one butcher's shop, a small Shire Council office, a small police station, an Elders store, a Dalgetty store, an open-air cinema, one public telephone, a wire fenced swimming pool in the harbour and a timber jetty.

---

2   In 1960 the Australian Government lifted an embargo on iron ore exports that it had held in place for two decades, because of concerns the mineral was in short supply.

A local population of Aborigines lived on the 1 Mile Reserve, located out of town. Tony said that most of them received a fortnightly pension from the Government, which unfortunately, got spent on grog and gambling. He had been waiting at the airport and drove us into town across a causeway that spanned four and a half miles of tidal flats. He told us that it flooded twice each year due to king tides.

As we got closer towards the town, I noticed how much junk there was on either side of the road: tin cans, bottles, rusty cars and smashed caravans. The road was a single lane and passing traffic had to move off the bitumen and onto the dirt. We were driving along Hunt Street when Tony pulled over and parked on the verge outside a house. We all piled out of the car and he introduced us to our new home.

It was one hundred and twenty degrees Fahrenheit, not a cloud in the sky, no breeze and as the red dust stirred up by his car settled, it clung to our damp skin. Hunt Street seemed really big; either side of the bitumen lane were wide, shallow dirt gutters that sloped up to level out where they met the front of the houses—I saw many times in the following years why those gutters were so wide.

Tony's house looked like a fortress. The first thing I noticed were large panels of full-height metal louvres that protected all of the windows; these were on steel frames bolted to the outside walls. In the front, a set of wooden steps lead up to an enclosed corner verandah and the main door. All around the verandah were full-width panels of corrugated iron sheeting; these were swung open and propped up with struts. Tony said they closed and bolted them during the cyclone season. The outside, which was probably painted white at one stage, was a light pink; I ran my fingers along the louvres and found them coated with fine red dust. The house was a basic, simple box with a low pitched corrugated iron roof. Raised up about three feet on metal stumps it had a small patch of grass in the front yard, several good sized trees and the property was enclosed by a metal framed wire fence. Along side of the front gate was a rusty forty four gallon drum; the rubbish bin. As I looked across the street I could see that many of the houses were up on stumps and some had metal louvres too; that was intriguing.

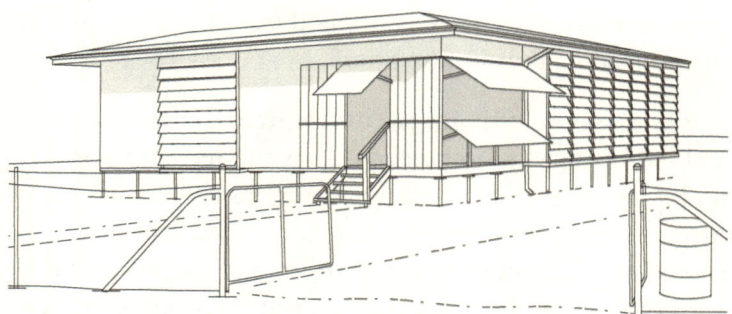

The Wiles' House, Hunt Street.

It was a Housing Commission property and we were sharing it with Tony, his wife Jean, their two adolescent boys and young daughter. There was a combined lounge/dining room, three bedrooms, a small kitchen, one toilet and one bathroom. We were given a small bedroom, there were no beds and we were all to sleep on the floor; Molly and I quickly realised there were going to be difficulties.

As promised, Keith Wiles offered me a job taxi driving that paid twenty five pounds a week, but I needed an Australian Driving License to work. I took Tony's car and visited the town's one policeman for a driving test—he handed me a letter, asked me to drive around the corner and post it for him, and then come back. That was it and I passed! Unfortunately for me, there was a month's waiting period while the paperwork was sent down to Perth to be processed and then returned, and I had to find some other work. Mt. Goldsworthy had an office in Port Hedland; so the same day, I applied for any labouring job that they might have on their books.

Within a few days, I was taken-on to labour for a drilling gang who were working on Finucane Island, located across the harbour from Port Hedland. The mining company wanted to test and find out if the island's sand would support the weight of stockpiling iron ore, brought in from Mt. Goldsworthy, while waiting for shipment.

Each day, at daybreak, we rowed the three quarter mile across to Finucane Island in a wooden boat—there were two drillers and two labourers—and carried our gear over to the drill site. My main job was handling the steel cases, which were fitted into the drill hole to stop it collapsing. We had to knock off around eleven o'clock because the steel became too hot to handle, and the drill rig's diesel motor overheated. We all rowed back to Port Hedland and the two drillers went straight to the Pier Hotel; I would slip home for a cup-of-tea and a sandwich with Molly. Around two o'clock in the afternoon we would meet back at the jetty, row out to the island and resume, working until dark. Over the next month we moved the rig, metal pipes and all its gear, by hand, to various locations on the island.

During my first week of work the weather deteriorated as Tropical Cyclone Lisa swept in from the Indian Ocean and then blew-out about fifty miles offshore, near the town of Karatha, which is located one hundred and twenty miles to the southwest of Port Hedland. A few days later, Betty, who had come ashore near Darwin in the Norther Territory, roared along on a southeasterly path and nearly made it all the way to Broome. While neither of the cyclones made a direct hit on Port Hedland their effect on the town was significant, with heavy cloud, high winds, driving rain and some flooding.

In the front of the Wiles' house is a tall tree; it's in the corner next to the driveway. The wind is hitting the tree hard and bending it over. When the tree bends, the earth heaves and cracks open as its roots hang on. The wind is trying to pull the tree out of the ground and its roots are trying to keep it in the ground. If it comes down, it could crash into the house or fall on the car.

Finucane Island was about two miles wide, one mile across and uninhabited; it was pristine. On the white sandy beaches lived a variety of seashells and some were very large. One day I brought home an eighteen inch long Bailor Shell, with beautiful copper coloured markings. To retain the shell's gloss, the animal inside had to be removed before it died. Tony showed Stephen and I how to hook the animal and then suspend the shell until it fell free, under its own weight. It got quite smelly and the bull ants eventually found it. One morning I found the empty shell on the ground and thoroughly cleaned it out; Molly put the beautiful Bailor in our room; one of our very few ornaments.

The children had to go to school and Molly enrolled them at Port Hedland Junior High School; there were mixed classes of both white children and Aboes. Stephen and Karen, coming from England, were eighteen months in advance of the other students and rarely progressed at all. The school was close enough so that they could walk there and Molly took them in each morning, both wearing their new school uniforms. She made them wear shoes on the first day, which turned out to be a novelty as everyone else wore rubber thongs; shoes were worn on sports days and the Aboes generally played in bare feet.

It's our first day at school and Mum is taking us to the office. She talks with the people there and then says she will come back and pick us up at three o'clock in the afternoon, when school is finished for the day. It's pretty lonely here without Mum and Karen is holding my hand; I'm glad she is.

A lady is taking us to our classrooms; I go in first. The lady talks to Karen, holds her hand and then they go off to find Karen's room. The teacher is telling the class my name and that I come from England. She says I don't have to wear closed shoes and can wear thongs like the other children; then I sit at a desk and class begins.

The first lesson is English and we go around the room spelling different words; I know all of them and spell

them in my head. When it's my turn the class looks
at me and a few laugh when I speak. The teacher says
well done and I sound very British; they all laugh. My
ears feel really hot and I know they are red; I'm glad
it's the next boy's turn.

I listen closely to the other children; to how they
speak Australian. The white children speak fast and
their voices go up at the end of each sentence, like a
question; the Aborigine's voices sound higher, they
use simpler words and are not so good at spelling.
If I speak more like an Australian then I won't get
laughed at.

At lunch time I go downstairs and sit with the other
children, under the school where it's shaded. A native
boy sits next to me and asks where England is. His
name is Jimmy. He is skinny and quick, like me.
He says they play marbles and if I get some I can
play. I have a bag full at home and will bring them
tomorrow; I like marbles. We eat our sandwiches
together. The bell is ringing.

Molly was trying to make the house work and, at first,
cooked in the kitchen with Jean to feed both families;
all eating at once. That turned out to be a shambles so
they worked out that Jean would feed her family first
and then Molly fed our family. It was very cramped
with four adults and five children all living under
one roof; tempers became frayed and both adults and
children were edgy as we moved through a difficult
time.

Russel is wrestling me; fighting me. Mr. Wiles is
standing by watching and laughing to himself, and

Mum is peering out the door at us. We roll around in the front yard, in the dirt. I'm not sure what to do. I'm lying on my tummy and he is on my back pulling my head up. My spine feels like it will break. I can hardly breathe. Maybe I'm dying. I'm very scared. Mr. Wiles says something and he gets off. I roll away and get up. He is on me again and I fight to keep my feet. I am not going down in the dirt again. I hit him in the face. He hits my shoulder. We tussle. I'm crying. I have never had a fight before.

Mum comes over, pulls us apart and takes me inside. She is worried that I'm crying and the others will hear. She is embarrassed. The other boy is not crying. I try to cry less and choke it down. I sob as she cleans me up in the bath tub. I hate this house, I hate these people and I hate this place. She gets me into some clean clothes. Later, I come out of our room. The two brothers snigger. I can't look at them. Mr. Wiles says to Mum that it's good for boys to fight. It doesn't seem good to me.

Then Mr. Wiles looks at Russell, and points at me with his finger. Russell comes over and holds out his hand. I know he doesn't mean it. I look him in the face and we shake. Mr. Wiles nods and smiles. So, that's it. All done. Now, it seems, we are all friends again. How does that work?

Stephen Outram

Twenty Five Pounds

A Short Story

If you drove from Perth to Port Hedland in 1965,
you would cover six hundred miles of bitumen road
and another six hundred miles of graded dirt road.
Depending on when the roads were last graded, you
might encounter vast stretches of corrugation in the
road's surface that would violently shake everything in
the car. Flooding and washouts during the rainy season
were common, as were the huge plumes of fine red
dust that rose high into the sky and tailed every vehicle
when it was dry. On a good trip the drive would take a
couple of days, with a stopover in Canarvon.

I wondered, if I had hitchhiked to Perth to take my
driving test and then driven back, would I have gotten
my license quicker? It took a month, and more, but my
driving licence finally arrived! I quit the Finucane job
and went to see Keith Wiles. He explained the fares
and charges, showed me the car and I became a taxi
driver starting the next day. The car was a white Ford
Falcon, four door with red vinyl interior and a powerful
six cylinder motor. Keith had an account with the local
petrol station so I could fill up when required. I got to
take the Ford home at night and had to check in with
Keith daily to hand over the money and see if there
were any bookings. I lasted just two weeks in the job
and must have been the shortest term taxi driver on

record!

I was so bored sitting in the taxi from eight in the morning until midnight. The town was small, the distances were small and most of the money taken was from the Aboes; driving them from one of the town's pubs out to their reserve. And most of the time the fare was covered with a, "Will you put it on the slate, mate." request i.e. to be paid when their fortnightly cheque came in; which required a good system of record keeping on my part to keep track of it all.

During my two long weeks working for Port Hedland Taxis, there were two interesting fares, both took me out to the Marble Bar area.

The Wine Rep.

A visiting wine representative wanted to go to the town of Marble Bar, which was about one hundred and twenty miles away; a good three hour drive. I knew it would be a valuable experience for me, learning to handle dirt roads at speed, and I took the fare.

All of the roads linking Port Hedland to other towns were made of dirt. They were simply cut out of the natural, scrubby bush by a grader and then maintained by regrading them from time-to-time. When the roads could not be fixed anymore, a new road was graded alongside the old one, which was reclaimed by the bush over time. Creek crossings were often done by laying in several concrete pipes to channel the water and packing dirt over the top; these primitive causeways would wash out during the rainy season and be repaired later in the year.

After some use, the graded dirt surface became corrugated. Drivers had to learn to quickly get the car up to a fair speed, so that the tyres would hit only the tops of the corrugations; this would smooth out the ride. The idea of a fair-speed varied depending on how much the road was used and regrading intervals; and until you got the speed right, the car seemed like it was shaking to pieces! This type of driving created a floating, drifting sensation as the car's tyres were, literally, in space for most of the time. It was like aquaplaning across water though this was 'corraplaning!' If you weren't paying attention, the car would slowly drift across the road towards the edge, and the gutter. Any panicked, jerky steering corrections would cause swerving, loss of control and sometimes an unplanned excursion into the surrounding bush. Driving at speed on dirt roads was an art to be mastered.

The fare was booked for Monday and we set off early in the morning. I had decided to take Stephen for a treat and some company on the way home; he wouldn't miss much at school. Stephen was in the back and the rep got in next to me. We headed out of Port Hedland along Wilson Street and turned west along the highway; just after Tabba Tabba Creek I found the small rusty sign to Marble Bar and turned right.

The further we drove, the hotter it got. All of the windows were wound down, dash vents full open and fine red dust swirled throughout the car. I quickly got the hang of driving on dirt but four tyres, constantly hitting the corrugations, made a steady drumming sound and we talked loudly to be heard over all the din.

I can't talk to my Dad and the man because it's too

60

loud in the car. And it's hot and windy. At least the flies are getting blown out. It's easier to sit and look out of the window. I see a couple of kangaroos; they are not moving, just standing under a gum tree. They are smart—too hot to be jumping around. There's an emu and he's not moving much either. I wonder, do they get bored out here? We're slowing down. There's a creek.

We came to the Shaw River crossing, a causeway where water was flowing over the road; I slowed right down as we drove through, listening to the water swish around our tyres. There was a good sized pool that had formed on the lee side; I pulled over and asked the others if they fancied a swim. My passenger, already a bit red-faced from the heat and wearing a coating of fine dust, liked the idea; Stephen was already out of the car!

We took off all of our clothes and waded into the water. It was amazingly good to sink down out of the heat. No one spoke for a while, just cooling down and listening to the gurgle of the water as it came over the causeway. We were probably the only humans for miles and miles. We stayed for half an hour, dried off in the sun and then resumed our journey much refreshed.

Marble Bar is famous for its gold, the Iron Clad Hotel, marble and being incredibly hot; it's known as the hottest place in the world. In 1923, the town set a world record for one hundred and sixty days at, or above, one hundred degrees Fahrenheit—believe me when I tell you that I was in no doubt!

I dropped the Wine Rep. off at the hotel, collected my ten pound fare and then Stephen and I explored the small town. We found our way to a quarry where marble had been mined, and when I splashed the rocks with water their colours were magnificent.

We're in a quarry. I can feel the heat bouncing off the rocks at me. The rocks are all lines, stripes with different colours: browns, reds, greys, whites. Dad is putting water on the rocks. Wow! I can really see the colours much brighter now. He says that it's called marble and men mined it here, and that's why the place is called Marble Bar.

After a good look around we headed back to Port Hedland. I dropped Stephen off at the house and went into town to finish my shift. He would be long in bed by the time I got home at midnight.

An Old Gate

My second out-of-town trip was at night, which was very different to driving in the daylight. A lady wanted to be returned to her husband; they lived at a small gold mine located eleven miles outside of Marble Bar. She had just come out of Port Hedland's hospital and I was to pick her up at the Pier Hotel at 8:00 p.m. When I arrived she smelt strongly of alcohol and must have downed several brandies for the trip. She got in the back and we sped out of town.

The danger of night driving in the Australian bush was, of course, the kangaroos. These large, nocturnal animals could become transfixed by a car's headlights and often jump at the last moment; sometimes smashing through the windscreen and landing in the back seat. We certainly had our share of 'roos that night, running across the road in front of the car.

Half way to Marble Bar it started to rain and got very heavy, making it hard to see very far ahead in the headlights. We pressed on at a slower speed and a few miles out of Marble Bar turned off the road down a track. Coming to a crossroad I took notice of an old timber gate; I looked back visualising the way we had come. My Dad, driving in London, told me to always notice the unusual: a church, a letter box, a tree, something to use in retracing our steps. He was so right and I still do it now. The downpour continued strongly but, eventually, we found the gold mine. The lady went in to their shack to wake her husband up and got the eleven pound fare so I could be paid.

My return journey was even more difficult as much of the track was under water. It continued to rain hard and sometimes half the car was underwater. I was quite frightened. All I had with me was a gallon of water for the radiator. Eventually I came to the crossroads, which were completely underwater too; all I could see was water. Then I spotted the gate, pointing me to the way home. I got back to Port Hedland at three o'clock in the morning; very grateful to be there and slipped into bed with Molly for a few hours sleep. I started work again at 8:00 a.m.

The way Keith Wiles divided the fares up was: a third to the owner, a third to run the car and a third to the driver. For my seven hour, two hundred and fifty mile drive I received three pounds and thirteen shillings. Twenty five pounds a week did not seem so attractive any more. At the end of two weeks as a taxi driver I went in and saw Keith, quit the job and then signed on to become a wharfie!

63

On the Docks

Work, Eat, Sleep, Work

Port Hedland was supplied by cargo vessels that arrived every two to three weeks on their journey north from Perth, sailing all the way up to Darwin in the Northern Territory. They stopped off at all ports delivering every conceivable item. On the return trip, these coastal boats would pick up cargo that needed to be sent south.

The ships would come in from the northeast at high tide to slip across Port Hedland's massive reef system, then hug the mainland avoiding Finucane Island's horn-like sandbar guarding the entrance to the harbour, and on to dock. The jetty was a substantial timber construction designed to take the weight of locomotives or large trucks that would drive out for loading or unloading. From the mainland, the jetty took the shape of the letter Y; its two angled arms were capped by a long dock, which created a triangle of water in the centre. At some point the jetty's centre had been lined with steel mesh, presumably for safe swimming, but no one used it except the many fish that could be seen on a clear day or when the tide stilled.

I go fishing at the jetty with Jimmy; he's an Aboriginal boy I met at school. Dad is there working a lot. There are so many fish. I can see them swimming around the big posts, under the jetty in the shade and in the middle part—we call that part The Aquarium. I have fishing line wound around a Coca Cola bottle with hook and sinker. Sometimes we fish with a jag hook that has three spikes. The hook gets lowered slowly down into a big shoal of fish and when they settle, jerk up fast; sometimes I get a fish on every spike. I love fishing.

When a ship came into port, one, two or three gangs of wharfies may have been required to unload it; depending on the size of the ship and its cargo. Each gang had twelve members, including a leader known as the Topman. A schedule was posted on a notice board at the office, with the ship's name, time of arrival and the gangs who would be working on it. Most of the wharfies had other jobs, but the ships always got top preference and were worked on until all of the cargo was discharged.

My pay, as a wharfie, was one and a half pounds an hour. There were penalty rates depending on when we worked and meals were provided. The ships always came and went on the high tide and could arrive at two o'clock in the morning, or any time. If you were willing to work, the money worked too. I was willing and worked every shift I could get.

I managed to get a position with the third gang and set about learning the job of a wharfie. The gang's hierarchy consisted of the topman who directed two winchmen, another two men worked on the trucks unloading the cargo and there were seven in the ship's hold. Winchmen operated the ship's winches that fed huge steel cables up to derricks; these swung out from the ship and over the jetty, lifting cargo up out of the hold to waiting trucks or visa versa. Those of us that worked in the sweltering holds would apply slings or nets to lift the cargo out, or guide the cargo and release the slings when it was lowered into the ship. It was hard physical work, often in extreme temperatures, but I was toughening up, getting fit and my pale English skin had turned a rich nut brown.

Another type of cargo we had to load was manganese, which was used in industry to harden steel. Woody Woody mine was established about four hundred kilometers from Port Hedland and run by Don Rhodes; it was out past Marble Bar along the Oakover River. Trucks of varying capacity were used to transport the ore; they were rated at twenty five, fifty or ninety tons— the largest was a road train with prime mover and several bogies. The trucks could only be driven at night, because the extreme day-time temperatures caused their tyres to puncture. So, night time driving was the game, which meant all night shifts for me.

Truck drivers were paid based on the tonnage of ore they delivered to Port Hedland. New drivers would always overload their trucks to get more money, but often spent that money by the side of the road on repairs. Manganese was stockpiled in Port Hedland and when a ship arrived the ore was loaded into kibbles, which were large, steel, cylindrical buckets with two eyelets welded at the top and one at the bottom. Each kibble held two tons of ore and arrived at the jetty on a flat-bed semitrailer, carrying 10 kibbles. The winches lifted a kibble across to the ship and a hook was attached to the bottom eyelet on a fixed length of steel; when the kibble was lowered into the hold, it would tip and spill the ore out. As the ore dropped a huge cloud of black manganese dust exploded upwards out of the hold; at the end of a shift, everybody and everything was covered in black dust.

A tally of the number of kibbles dumped would be collected by the man directing the trucks on and off the jetty, and that was the record used to determine tonnages shipped and monies paid.

I've found a way to climb under the jetty; I can get right under. The beams are really wide so I can crawl along them. When the tide is going out quickly, these fish called Grunters swim really fast in the rushing current, around the posts. They will chase anything that looks like food. I have a small piece of shiny metal tied to my line, near the hook. It flashes in the tumbling water and I can catch them. When they come up out of the water they make a grunting noise.

When a cargo ship was emptied, its cargo was stored in a goods shed until collected; I managed to get extra work in the shed as a tallyman. All items that were claimed got a receipt and then the receipt details had to be entered in a Bill of Loading ledger; this method ensured that all goods were in the correct port and it recorded that they were collected.

In between ships and the goods shed work, I managed to get a job in our local Elders store putting up new shelving to begin with and later I helped out by serving in the shop. Elders carried every conceivable item imaginable to supply goods required by all the surrounding stations[1]; everything from saddles to clothes pegs. They even had a special medicine corner to help with hangovers and its associated bumps, scrapes and bruises: Dr. Watt's Liver Medicine, Dr. Paul's Kidney Medicine, ointment for burns, pains and headaches.

Early on Saturday morning, fresh fruit and vegetables were flown up from Perth; there were boxes and boxes of them. All of the fresh produce had to be unpacked, sorted and put on the shelves before opening time, at nine o'clock in the morning. At nine sharp, all of the women in Port Hedland descended on the store and it was a frantic three hours of retail bedlam until everything was totally gone. I made sure I put a box away, before we opened, to take home for the family.

Working three jobs came at a cost and I didn't see much of Molly or the children. My life had become work, eat, sleep, work and more work.

I take the fish I catch, the good ones, home to Mum. I have to clean out all the guts and scale them, then wash them clean with water. She takes them but I know she doesn't really like them—all raw and slippery with their eyes looking. Sometimes she cooks them. When I get a big one and give her just the fillets, then she likes that much better. Her mouth kind-of tightens when she picks them up. Ha! Mums are funny sometimes.

---

1   Outside of Port Hedland were several large pastoral properties; stations producing wool, livestock and other goods that they transported into town and ship out from the docks. Some of their names were: Boodarie, Pippingarra, Strelley and Carindi.

When Dad is waiting for a new cargo ship to come in at the wharf, he does some fishing. I know when he's caught some because there is fish in the refrigerator when I get up. When he is not working, he will cook the fish for Mum, but mostly she cooks. When I'm down at the jetty fishing, sometimes I see him on the trucks or the boat working. If he sees me, he always waves.

Chicken Coup Bedroom

A New Home

We had been living in Tony and Jean's house for about six months when they received a letter from the Housing Commission stating, "One house, one family." It looked like we had been dobbed in! Most likely by someone who was waiting for a house! This created a problem for us as there was no rental accommodation in Port Hedland. We decided to put our names on the waiting list for our own Housing Commission house, but that could take years as people tended to stay in these properties for a long time.

Even though our current situation, sharing with the Wiles family, was cramped and not ideal, we had all adapted and were making the best of it. Looking back though, this disruption came at a good time as both families were unhappy with the lack of space.

I talked our accommodation situation over with the gang on the wharf and a single bloke, Tim, said he had a ten foot caravan sitting at the bottom of his garden. He told me, jokingly, that it hadn't been used for a hundred years! There was a shower, toilet and laundry close by in a detached shed, and we could rent the caravan from him.

I took Molly for a look. We had lived in caravans

in England and were familiar with the lifestyle. The caravan stood under a big shady tree that would shelter us from the sun, and close by was an uninhabited chicken coop! The caravan was complete, dry inside and the gas cooker worked. We ran a power cable from the laundry and all the lights turned on. Although it was pretty filthy from disuse, we knew it would clean up well and decided to take it.

Molly and I cleaned it out one afternoon, scrubbing everything from top to bottom and airing out all of the seat cushions and mattress. We dragged the chicken coup over, closer to the caravan. It was made up of a lightweight timber frame covered all over with chicken wire, and had a wire-mesh door that opened and closed on a latch. We scrubbed it too, raked out the dirt floor, made up two fold-up type beds and placed them inside, for the kids to sleep in. I got some plywood sheeting from work and fixed a makeshift roof; if it rained hard then we could bring Karen and Stephen in with us.

When it was all ready, we moved out from the Wiles' house and into 76 Kingsmill Street our new place—a clean caravan complete with one chicken coup bedroom and all sited under a great shady tree. Perfect!

We've all been sleeping in the same small bedroom at the Wiles' place; it's strange now, to have so much space. I like it! I can't hear Dad breathing anymore. Karen is just over there in her bed. If I slide over to the side of my bed I can see the sky and some stars. It's a funny bedroom with the chicken wire but it feels safe; the door is closed and nothing will get in. The caravan's lights have gone out. Mum says, "Good night" from the door. She sat with Karen for a while until Sis' went to sleep. She told us that she would only close the caravan's screen door, and we can call out to her if we need to.

It's dark but I can still see a lot. I can hear the tree. The leaves are moving; rustling. What are they saying? It has a big strong trunk and there's a car tyre hanging down on some rope. I'll swing in that tomorrow. It's fun out here; it's like camping in a forest. And the bathroom's over there behind me. Funny. Yawn. I like the tree.

Molly was a qualified hairdresser and had done salon work in England. The children were gone for most of the day in school and we talked about getting her some work; something to do during the day.

She had noticed that Port Hedland didn't have any women's hairdressing services in town and the men got their hair cut in the pub. A few times each year, a hairdresser drove from Perth to Darwin, stopping off at all of the towns along the way. She would do styled haircuts and perms, and make a fortune; she was always booked months in advance. We didn't have any facilities but I put a notice up in town that Molly was offering women's hairdressing under the tree at 76 Kingsmill Street. Several town's women came over to see her right away and the word quickly got around.

Molly didn't realise it at the time but she made history under that big shady tree. The town's women came and sat underneath it and while they chattered away were transformed by her hand. And as often happens with great hairdressers, her clients lightened their load of life's troubles and usually left with big smiles on their faces.

Molly became Port Hedland's first resident hairdresser; more importantly though, she was beginning to create a place for herself in the community, and there was much more to come for my lovely wife.

Stephen Outram

School

Port Hedland Junior High School

From 1956 to 1969 the school in Acton Street
functioned as a junior high school providing children's
education ranging from Year Eight to Year Twelve.
In 1970 it became a high school and then in 1971,
Hedland Senior High School. Karen and Stephen's
first couple of years were a doddle as their English
education placed them ahead of the local children. In
addition, allowance was made in the curriculum for the
Aboe's children who often found white fella's teachings
unfamiliar.

Our school is near the ocean; Karen and I go to
the same school but we do different classes. The
classrooms are upstairs and underneath is where we
have lunch and play, in the shade. The main buildings
are in a U shape and in the middle is the parade
ground, where we sing the anthem, God Save the
Queen, in the morning. A new wing is being built at
the school but it's not ready yet.

Behind the library are basket ball courts and down
the back is the sport's ground. I play softball and do
running races.

We have to drink milk in the morning. At my school
in England the milk was in small glass bottles, and we

would take off the silver top and just drink it, but in Port Hedland the milk is in triangular shaped cartons and it's frozen! So, we play a game and guess which corner of the triangle has the creamy bit and then cut off the corner with scissors, but then we have to wait until the ice melts to get it.

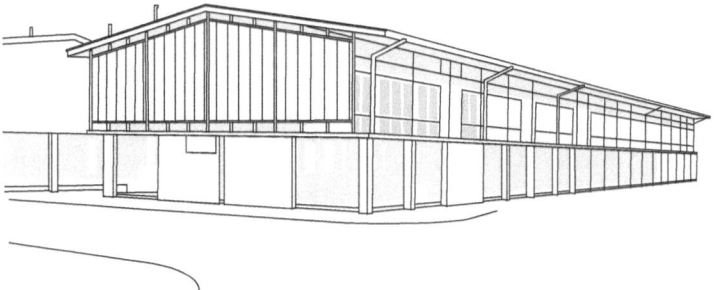

Port Hedland Junior High School, North Wing

The teachers are nice and I get good grades in spelling and maths. Sometimes I sing with the choir at assembly. We get to go to Mt. Goldsworthy school on sports day and swim in their pool. I won at breast stroke and came third in overarm.

We swim a lot in the wire pool down near the jetty, in the harbour. There's not that much water in it at low tide, but it gets pretty full at high tide. The wire keeps the sharks out. A sea snake came swimming through the other day, right between us; good thing the tide took him away and he just swam right through the wire on the other side and kept on going. One day they brought a shark's teeth in to school!

"Schoolchildren from the Port Hedland,
Western Australia, Junior High School—
Darny Zorancic, 9 and Eric Lockyer, 15—are
all smiles as they examine the jaws of a 9 ft
shark, but the fisherman's memento is a grim
warning. The shark, caught alongside the town's
enclosed swimming pool, was displayed at local
schools."— The Canberra Times. Tuesday, 13
July 1965

My school uniform is grey shorts and a grey shirt, and
Karen's dress is light green with small white squares all
over it. In England I had a jacket, tie and cap to wear;
I'm glad we didn't bring those with us. Some children
don't wear shoes; we wear rubber thongs to school
but they get into trouble when they have bare feet.

I play marbles at lunchtime with the other boys.
We use catseyes and boulders and peewees, and play
along the side of the building in the dirt. Sometimes
our games go really long and we have to run to class
when the bell goes. I'm pretty good and have a big
bag of marbles. When someone wins they get to keep
the other boy's marbles; even the special ones like
peewees and boulders.

I can see the ocean from some of the classrooms and
the big ships come in. My Dad works on the ships at
the jetty. I can't see him from school though.

One of the teachers got a bunch of us kids together
and we put pig's poo into a forty four gallon drum
and mixed it with water and hay. I had to go down
every day, take the lid off and stir it up. It was very
smelly. Then, when it was ready we planted banana

76

plants in the ground and put on the fertilizer that we made. We have to water them and fertilize them and when they grow big we are going to eat the bananas; I hope all of the poo has gone by then

I've had one fight at school, but we didn't get caught by a teacher; the bell rang and we had to stop and go to class. And I've been to see the principal once when an older boy was picking on me and I got angry and left the school to get away. I didn't get the cane but Mum found out about it.

I walk home from school with Karen along Acton Street; sometimes we walk along the beach. Mum is home when I get there; often she is working and fixing up the women's hair, so I have to keep quiet and do my homework. Dad works a lot so I don't see him as much as Mum.

Stephen Outram

Goldsworthy 1 & 2

English Electric, Rocklea

The freighter I. G. Nicholson docked at Port Hedland in December 1965, carrying a special cargo. In its hold were a pair of brand new diesel-electric locomotives that had been manufactured by the English Electric Company in Rocklea, Queensland. These were to be employed on the new railway line being constructed between Mount Goldsworthy and Finucane Island.

Working on the wharf, I was able to arrange access for the kids and took them down into the ship's hold. They were excited to see the two sister locomotives, with their gleaming yellow and white paint jobs. Each machine had a plaque mounted on their cab displaying the name: *Goldsworthy 1* and *Goldsworthy 2*, in bold white lettering. Sitting side-by-side and waiting patiently, they filled the ship's hold. Stephen and Karen climbed on board the locomotives and even went inside one of the cabins.

We are down the steps and in the ship's hold. There are two yellow trains down here but they don't have any wheels. Oh! The wheels are over there, they haven't been put on yet. Dad says they are locomotives and we can get on them. I'm climbing up a steel ladder and standing on the walkway; Karen is up here too. Dad calls out and takes some photographs; we pretend that we work on the trains and salute. I open a steel door and go inside the cabin; I'm the train driver. The driver can't see straight out front because a big motor is in the way, and I have to look out of the side windows. The train is really nice; it's called *Goldsworthy 1* and the other is *Goldsworthy 2*.

The locomotives weighed seventy two tons each and were far too heavy for the ship's winches. Arrangements had been made for Utah Dredging Company's floating crane, the third largest in the world, to off-load them. I went down the next day to watch the unloading. Utah's barge-crane pulled up along side the freighter—it was rated at just over seventy six tons lifting capacity—and was secured with heavy lines; all was ready.

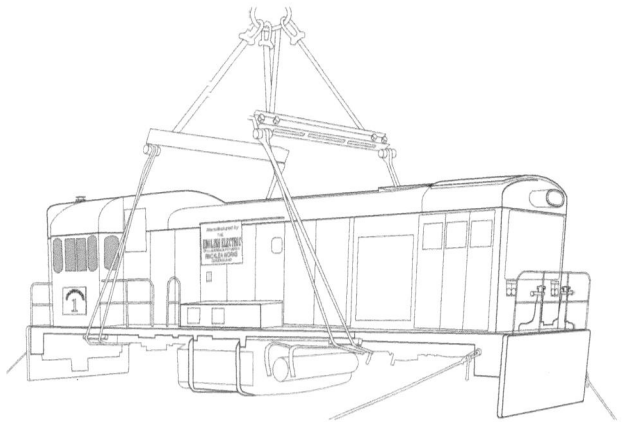

Goldsworth 1 being lifted.

The barge's huge derrick swung over the ship and a massive hook was lowered down into the hold where lifting slings were attached. When all was ready and with a hand-signal from the dogman, the crane's motor roared and took up the strain; black smoke spewed out of its exhaust pipe, high into the air. As Goldsworthy 1 came up, off the hold's floor, the barge became forward-loaded and its nose sunk dramatically into the water; to within a few inches of the deck line. Seventy two tons of dead weight started to swing across the hold but was held by strong stay lines. It was a tense moment and I'm sure the crane driver's heart jumped in his chest. Mine did! Inch-by-inch the great hook rose out of the hold and the locomotive's white roof caught the sun. When it cleared the ship's rails, the driver eased his load over the side. He gradually positioned it more central to the barge, which slowly righted itself and eventually, the locomotive was lowered and placed neatly on-deck.

It was quite a sight to see a fifty foot locomotive come up out of the hold, hang high over the ship, swing out over the water and then be lowered safely onto the barge. Over several days, the barge unloaded both locomotives, their bogies and gear, transporting each of them over to Finucane Island where they would begin work on the Mount Goldsworthy railway line.

Later, in 1966, a further six locomotives were delivered to Port Hedland by ship, though these were different as they were based on the WAGR H Class design; [1]Goldsworthy 1 and 2 were both K Class units. With the arrival of these two powerful machines, I had witnessed a piece of history and was beginning to see a little of the future and get a sense of the change that the town would undergo. The scale of works, general engineering and equipment for handling iron ore at

---

1   Of the two locomotives, only "Goldsworthy 2" has survived; it's displayed at Port Hedland in Don Rhodes Mining and Transport Museum.

Port Hedland was huge and would increase. In the years to come world records were made, broken and reset for longest train, heaviest train, shipping tonnage and iron ore throughput; but that is another story and one for the future.

The Dutchman

Christmas 1965

About halfway through 1965 a dredge appeared in
the harbour; the Japanese vessel Alameda was one of
the most powerful dredges in the world. Its job was to
extend the harbour and clear a channel through the
reefs, some seven miles out to sea, which would allow
large ore carriers to access Port Hedland at any time.
This was regarded as the biggest dredging operation
ever undertaken in Australia and a USA company, Utah
Mining and Construction, had the job. A new iron ore
mine, Mt. Goldsworthy, was being built and would be
transporting iron ore to Port Hedland's Finucane Island
via railway line where it would be stockpiled ready for
loading. The demand for the port to handle greater
capacity ships and increase exports was growing.

With the rise and fall of tides it was possible to walk
across an exposed sandbar to Finucane Island, on the
low. In fact, pearling luggers used to beach their boats
on the sandbar to do maintenance. With the dredging
work, that natural causeway would be cut away. The tide
levels in the area varied enormously from neaps to king
tides. During neaps, the tide only rose and fell three
feet, spring tides could rise from thirteen to eighteen
feet, which was a huge volume of water moving in and
out; and on king tides the sea level rose up to twenty
four feet, twice each year. The channel dredging had to

reach deep enough to handle the giant iron ore carriers, and allow for these huge tidal variations.

Today there were these huge explosions. Boom! Boom! Dad said they were dynamiting the reef to get the channel through for the big ore boats. I went down to the beach and there were hundreds, maybe thousands (we haven't learnt to count that far yet) of dead fish. All kinds, grunter, rock cod, brim, garfish. They are floating on top of the water and laying around on the beach. in amongst the mangroves. No one is picking them up; they will stink soon. A couple of booms and all the fish are dead; probably the crabs, cowrie shells and blue ring octopus too. The beach is like a graveyard. Is that why it's called Cemetery Beach? I pick up two brim from the water and take them home to Mum She asks, "Where did you get those?" and I tell her about all the dead fish. She says. "Take them back." and tells me to keep away from the beach. I guess there's not much point going fishing anyway.

While working as tallyman in the goods shed I met a Dutchman; his full name was Wimpy Noines but everyone knew him as Wimpy. He was the local bottler; there were no cans in Port Hedland and Wimpy used to collect all of the empty bottles every Saturday. He had a couple of old trucks, which also delivered cargo from the goods shed out into Port Hedland and its surrounding areas; business was growing and he needed a new driver. I left the tallyman's job and began driving his trucks.

Wimpy had built himself a house with two petrol pumps out front and had negotiated a contract to supply fuel to any government vehicle. His ambition was to expand the business by building a shop, and after I'd been working with him for a while he asked if I would help him. The deal was that if I helped him build the shop I could have a room in the back of it, which would be better than our caravan. The room could be our home and when we eventually left, he would convert it to a storage area for the shop. I agreed.

So, my main job was wharfie, then I drove trucks and delivered cargo and whatever time was left over after that was spent building a shop to get us better living conditions. The days and the weeks flew by.

Wimpy was married and had a son, about Stephen's age, but he didn't seem to be a particularly nice man; he was a bit gruff, rarely smiled and Molly didn't like him at all, but in November I got the shop finished. We said goodbye to the caravan, chicken coup bedroom and the big shady tree, and moved in to Wimpy's storeroom.

The new building was steel framed and sheeted with corrugated iron; the shop was located out front, facing the roadway, and our room at the rear. We had a space that measured six feet wide by eighteen feet long; it had a door, one glass louvred window, a sink, a power point and we shared a bathroom and toilet with Wimpy and his family. On the inside, the steel frame was exposed as there was no sheeting on the walls or ceiling, the floor was bare concrete and a solitary light bulb hung down from the roof; it was our second move and third home in Port Hedland.

Coming from a caravan, we didn't have much in the way of furniture; a couple of chairs and the children's fold-up beds. Molly and I scoured the town and managed to buy a double bed for us, one settee and a small Formica topped table with four chairs. I located a wooden box and we put that at one end of the room, covered it with some cloth and used it to hold a tape player, pictures, some odds and sods and our beautiful bailor shell from Finucane Island.

We put all the beds at the other end of the room, and Molly fashioned a curtain that we could pull across to provide a screen, while I slept during shift work. I installed a kitchen bench near the sink and we bought an old kerosene refrigerator to go next to it. Someone offered a cooker and I put a gas cylinder just outside the window and ran the connecting hose inside. We also had an aluminium, electric fry pan with a lid and that was used frequently. Molly found some mats to put down over the concrete floor and fitted fly wire and a curtain to the window. Our tin shed; our home, began to work!

Wimpy had agreed that Molly could continue her hairdressing business and she began receiving customers once again. He had fitted and stocked the shop and was open for business, and his shop benefited as more business came his way from Molly's clients. Wimpy had taken delivery of a batch of model ships and he came to see me. He asked if Stephen would build one of the models so he could display it in the shop's window; he would give Stephen two models, one to keep. Over dinner I asked Stephen if he would like to do that and he was very keen. I explained that Wimpy wouldn't give him his model, until he had completed the first one for display.

Mr. Wimpy has dropped in a model ship for me to build. It's a war ship, all grey with guns and pretty big too; eighteen inches long. Dad gave me some wood to put it all on. There's lots of pieces—all the ship's parts and some paint, brushes, a tube of glue and stickers. I've started it already and work on it as soon as I get home from school. Mum says I have to stop for dinner. It has drawings that show where all the parts go, and what to click or glue together. Soon I'll have it done and then I can get my own ship. Dad says it's looking really good. He was in the navy!

December came quickly and we were all very excited about celebrating our first Christmas in Australia. Most of the fun was in hiding the children's presents, without Stephen finding them in our small accommodation. We ended up hiding their gifts in Wimpy's shop and I snuck them in on Christmas Eve.

It's Christmas and we are all in bed. Karen and I hung up stockings on the end of our beds for Santa Clause to find and put the presents in. There's milk and cake in the fridge for him too. We left a little light on so Santa can see. When I look up over my covers I can see the room; I'm going to stay awake and see Santa when he comes.

Shhh! I can hear a noise. Someone is in our place. I'm scared. I'm excited. I keep my eyes closed in case he sees me looking. Someone is moving by my bed. My heart is pounding. I hear Mum say, "Oh, is that you Santa?" The fridge door opens, and closes. I hear the door click and then it's quiet. I peek out from under my covers but no one is there. The light clicks off and it's dark. Wow! I'm sure it was him. Santa was in our house!

Molly and I had started smoking; it had begun as a social thing and now we both smoked regularly. We liked Craven A cork tip and they cost three shillings and two pence a packet; occasionally I bought cigarillos, which were a thinner dark-papered smoke with a stronger taste. One day at home, while I was reading the newspaper, Stephen asked me if he could try a cigarette. It caught me by surprise but I didn't look up, acted totally disinterested and told him he could.

Dad has said that I can try his cigarettes. I've watched them smoking; it doesn't smell nice but looks like fun to blow the smoke out. I'm sitting on the box at the end of our room and the cigarette packet and matches are right next to me. I take a Craven A out of its packet, put it between my lips and light the match. I've watched Dad do it and he sucks the flame into the end of the cigarette to light it. Now it's smoking; I'm having a good look at the glowing end and then put the filter end in my mouth and suck in some smoke; then I blow it out. It tastes horrible, but I do it again and blow the smoke up towards the roof. I keep going and can see the smoke floating in the air.

Dad is still reading his paper and Mom is folding up the washing on their bed; I sit on the box and smoke the whole cigarette, then stub it out in the ashtray. Hmm. Well, I don't like cigarettes all that much. My mouth tastes bad. I tell Dad I'm going out to play; and he keeps reading and tells me to be home for lunch. Okay Dad. I go and rinse my mouth out with the hose outside it still tastes bad!

Topman

New Money

In February 1966, seven native animals appeared on
our coins as Australia began its conversion to decimal
currency and a new metric measurement system. The
familiar Queen's head was retained on all but the fifty
cent coin, but it was uncomfortable letting go of the
familiar pounds, shillings and pence; another tie with
England was being cut. The notes changed too, into
dollars: colourful one, two, five, ten, twenty and fifty
dollar notes began to circulate as the old pound notes
were traded in.

About this time I was offered the job of Topman. I
had worked in the ship's holds and then progressed
on to winchman; now, as Topman, I had my own gang
of twelve. My pay increased with the new role though
I didn't really have a good sense of it with the new
currency. For quite a while, everyone spent a lot of time
converting prices back to pounds, shillings and pence
so we knew what we were being paid, or what we were
paying when we bought something.

A new steel dock had been built over at Finucane Island
and with the completion of the Mount Goldsworthy
rail line, iron ore was being stockpiled on the other side
of the harbour. The first ore was delivered to the island
in May and shortly after, Alameda finished dredging

the channel. Harvey S. Mudd, a thirty thousand tonne ore carrier docked at Finucane and three weeks later, sitting much lower in the water, left the harbour full of Australian iron ore and headed for Japan. It was the first of many.

By now a greater number and variety of ships were calling into Port Hedland—everything came in by cargo ship to the old timber jetty where I worked and iron ore was loaded from the Finucane Island dock. A mining town was to be built near Mount Newman, four hundred and twenty kilometres away, including a railway connecting a new dock in the harbour. Roads, bridges, fuel depots, pipelines, homes, retail buildings and the like were going to be needed, and so the cement ships used to call.

Many thousands of bags of cement were packed loose in a ship's hold and to remove them, every forty kilogram bag had to be picked up and placed onto a timber palette, which was then hoisted up and loaded onto a flat-bed truck waiting on the wharf. There were two teams of men working either side of the hold, each team had to place twenty four bags onto a pallet and the pallets were hoisted alternatively; so there was a rhythm and a pattern to be maintained. The temperature in the hold often reached over forty degrees Celsius and our water-bags were constantly being replenished. The routine was to work the ship for sixteen hours, have a break for eight hours and then start all over again. I had an older partner, who was sixty five, and often had to lift many of the bags on my own so that we could keep up with the regular pattern of hoisting. Sometimes the bags broke or leaked and there was always fine concrete dust floating in the air. We looked like pale grey ghosts, streaked with sweat as we laboured in the heat.

By now nearly eighteen months had passed since we had arrived in Port Hedland; it was April 1966 and a welcome reprieve from the heat was easing in. Weather-wise, July through to late September was the best time of year as the nights were cool at twelve degrees Celsius and the temperature hovered around twenty two during the day; it was absolutely perfect! On from September, an intense dry heat built up to forty degrees or more, with cyclones in the summer months bringing horrendous winds, driving rain and widespread flooding.

Sometimes the cyclones tracked the Western Australian coastline and at other times they crossed and came inland. There seemed to be no logic to the way they moved and the best that weather forecasters could do was to guess where they were going. Tropical Cyclone Joan had come to visit in March the previous year and crossed south of Port Hedland near the town of Karatha, heading inland as far as Newman. Joan was rated Category 3, with winds gusting over two hundred kilometers per hour. Earlier in the year Lisa had blown herself out off the coastline but in April, Shirley crossed at Karatha and ran inland nearly all the way down to Geraldton.

I now knew why the Wiles' house had metal louvres fixed securely to the outside and why it was up on stumps. As we looked out of our door, the rain was horizontal. There were stories told of metal roofing sheets or fencing posts flying wildly through the air, and cars being stripped of their paint as the winds picked up sand from the beach and flung it at the unprotected vehicles parked in the street. The wide, street gutters that we had noticed when first arriving in Port Hedland were now full and overflowing with the massive deluge of rain dumped upon the town and surrounding areas. After the main storm had passed the Aboes would stand out in the streets, in the rain, and children played in the flooded areas, treating them like swimming pools.

Bang! There's a big noise and it wakes us all up. Dad goes outside in the rain to have a look. He comes back and says it's all right and we can all go back to sleep. Something just hit the roof and then blew off again. It's hard to sleep. The rain on our tin roof sounds like a thousand stones are hitting it, and the wind keeps screaming really high; even higher than the girls at school can scream.

The curtain around Mum and Dad's bed keeps getting sucked in and out; sometimes it goes high up near the roof. Mum gets up and ties it down with some string. Everyone is awake, lying in bed, listening to the cyclone. Thump! Something smaller hits our wall and makes me start. Soon it will be morning and I can go outside and see what has happened. I'm glad we have steel walls. I wonder if Port Hedland has blown away? Then I wouldn't have to go to school. What is the wind saying and why do girls scream the way they do?

As the coastal ships came and went I made friends with a steward named Robbie. One day while unloading his ship, the gang was having a tea break, Robbie was leaning over the rail and we got talking.

He had noticed my accent and asked what I was

91

doing out here in Port Hedland. I explained that we were British migrants trying to make a go of it here in Australia. He seemed interested and asked what I missed the most since coming out from England. I laughed and had to tell him that it was fresh milk! He grinned and told me that he could soon fix that.

Robbie led me into the galley and took a large stainless steel container out of the refrigerator. He tipped it up and very slowly, tantalizingly poured ice-cold, fresh, cow's milk into a large glass. Finally, having milked the moment for all it was worth, he handed me the glass and told me to try it. Did that milk taste good? Oh yes! You see, all we had in Port Hedland was powdered milk; it was fine but nothing like the real thing. We kept in touch each time his ship visited the town, and he proved to be a good friend over the next few years.

Water Ski Trip

A Notable Event

Several notable events occurred in Port Hedland during the first part of the 1966:

there was the normal armada of tropical cyclones—
Amanda, Lisa and Shirley;

Mount Goldsworthy's new railway line delivered its
first shipment of ore to Finucane Island on the first
of May,

in the harbour, Alemeda finished its dredging work
and opened way for the thirty thousand tonne ore
carrier, Harvey S. Mudd, to enter on May 27;

work began on an all-weather road to be
constructed between Canarvon and Port Hedland, a
nine year project;

and one month after its arrival, the Harvey S. Mudd
sailed with just under twenty five thousand tonnes
of Australian iron ore in its holds.

Another notable and memorable event was our first water skiing trip.

We had dropped in to see Tony and Jean for a visit and they invited us to a water skiing trip that they were planning, out at Finucane Island. Tony knew of a spot that was great for water sports and was taking some friends out for the afternoon. It seemed like it would be a lot of fun and I said that we'd love to go with them. We arranged to meet up with them on the following Saturday.

The day came around quickly enough and Tony picked us up at the wooden jetty in his boat; we set out for Finucane Island about eleven o'clock in the morning on a rising tide. The idea was to travel up a creek that on high tide, filled and connected the harbour to the open sea. There were two boats in our flotilla, Tony's four and a half metre and another smaller aluminium boat; a tinnie. Both were filled with adults, children, eskys, skis, surfboards and beach gear; it was going to be a fun day!

We crossed the harbour and headed towards the western side of the island; to the appropriately named Western Creek. Tony turned us north into the creek and soon we landed on a beautiful white sand beach; everyone piled out and began sorting the gear and getting a cold beer. Several colourful beach umbrellas went up, towels went down, eskys were placed in the shade of nearby bushes and someone began digging a trench in the sand to house a fire for the barbecue; the children headed straight for the water, but Tony called them back and told them to wait.

There were three families on the trip and soon the adults had everything unpacked. Tony and one of the men took both the boats out and began racing up and down the creek at top speed; they did this three or four times and then came back and beached the boats. Tony explained that they were scaring off any sharks that might have been lurking in the area, and now we could swim. I was only a little reassured, but everyone splashed happily into the water and there seemed to be some safety in numbers so I joined them. Glorious!

We had a great day with cold drinks, steaks sizzling on a hotplate, skiing and swimming in the clear waters, and a hilarious, impromptu football game on the beach with children and adults all running around yelling like crazy people. It was everything we had imagined an Aussy barby would be and more. In the afternoon, Molly mentioned that the tide was dropping but Tony said we would be okay and wanted to have one last ski. When he got back we packed everything into the boats again, and headed back towards the harbour.

It wasn't long before the loaded boat was bumping along the creek's sandy bottom and we realised that we were not going to get through into the harbour; the tide was running out fast and we had missed our chance. Tony turned around, back into deeper water, and told us that we'd just have to go around Finucane and come in via the main harbour entrance. That meant heading out into the open ocean, but Tony assured us it would be fine.

We made our way through the narrowing creek, finding its often illusive, deeper channel and with a magnificent sunset cheering us on motored out through the bar into the Indian Ocean, turning northeast and running parallel to Finucane's northerly beaches. The swell was moderate but we were running against the tide and wind; the smaller boat's motor began to falter and eventually stopped. Tony took it in tow and had to make regular stops as his motor began to overheat from hauling two boats, all the people and their gear.

It was very dark and there were no lights to be seen as Finucane shielded the town from us. Stephen was in the second boat; there was a surfboard laid across its prow and he was sitting on it, holding onto the boat's sides as it rolled in the swell. He must have gotten tired because the next time I looked he was lying on the surfboard. Molly saw him too, screamed out and told one of the adults to get the boy into the boat. She was very worried that he would slip into the water and become shark's bait. Some room was made and he curled up in the bottom of the boat, with a towel wrapped around him.

Over five hours later, we finally arrived at the most north-easterly point of Finucane Island and made a big sweeping turn towards the mainland, to avoid sandbars. The tide, which had begun to turn, picked us up and swept the two boats and their weary passengers into the harbour. There was a cheer and we finally made it back to the jetty at midnight. It seemed a long climb up the ladders and I was very grateful to step onto the jetty and feel solid wooden planks under my feet. We said good night and gathered up our gear. I counted four heads, including mine, and then drove us home to clean up and get some sleep.

Molly never forgave Tony his "one last ski," which put us all in a difficult situation. The unhappy vision of one of us being lost in Port Hedland's shark infested waters stayed with her for a very long time.

A Plot

So Far Out of Town

Port Hedland was growing fast, there was limited housing and despite there being wide open spaces all around the town, residential land was in short supply. The Shire Council responded by releasing a parcel of Crown Land, located one and a half kilometers out of town, near the Old Port Hedland Cemetery. Molly and I thought it would be a good idea to buy a plot and then build ourselves a house.

When we mentioned that Council was auctioning off the land, to people we knew, they scoffed and asked why on Earth would we want to live so far out of town?

Molly and I went to inspect the plots on offer and all there was to see were a series of pegs in the ground and some taller stakes marking out the area; the roads were simple, freshly graded dirt. We decided to have a go and chose a block on the corner of Brearley and Anderson Streets. I was working and so Molly went to the auction on her own. She bought number two Brearley Street for four hundred and sixty dollars. Things were looking up!

It's just flat dirt. There are no houses anywhere. Some wooden pegs have been put in the ground and Dad is showing us the four corners of the block. He gets us all to stand on the corners so we can see how big it

97

is. It looks too small for a house to go on. Who will be our neighbours? And how will I get to the wire swimming pool and to school? Will we be getting a car? There's an old cemetery over there; I'm taking a look. Old headstones, some graves have a small fence around them and others are just mounds. I can see the beach from here; it's close to the block. Mum's calling me. Time to go.

I began thinking about a house; what it might look like and what materials we would need to build it. I went and visited the block on my own and had a good look around; it had been a good choice. The block was on the lee side of a low hill that fronted Cemetery Beach, which would provide us with some shelter from onshore winds during the cyclone season. It was also relatively high ground with little chance of flooding during the wet, and we could have an on-ground concrete slab as the base. I had an idea, which would help us with the slab.

When I was unloading the cement ships at the wharf, I began asking their captains if I could sweep up any loose cement that had fallen from broken bags; most were happy to have their holds cleaned out and agreed. With each ship we cleared I worked on, shoveling the sweepings into a container; I used one of Wimpy's trucks and took it out to Brearley Street where I off-loaded the cement into forty four gallon drums that I'd collected. When the container was empty, I took the truck back to Wimpy's and then it was almost time to start another shift. Although it was extra work at the time, I knew it would pay off in a big way, in the future.

I calculated that I was going to need about fourteen

drums of cement for the footings and slab, and by the time I had finished up my wharf job as Topman, I had them all lined up in a row on site; each one had a piece of asbestos-cement sheeting on top weighed down with a rock. We were ready to start!

44 Gallons of Rubbish

Cleaning Up Port Hedland

The Shire Council had pinned a new note on their notice board,

> "For Tender. Contractor wanted to remove all household and commercial rubbish in the Port Hedland area. Four days a week. Shire Council will supply and maintain vehicle. Apply within."

A friend said that I ought to have a go at that!

I did some investigating and found out that the Council had paid two Aboes to do the job, but it wasn't getting done! During the run they would call in at the hotel and buy a flagon of wine, then head out to the rubbish dump and would not been seen for the rest of the day. So, Council was looking for a new crew. I worked it out that if I could get paid seventy dollars for working four days, then I would have some spare time to put towards building a house at Brearley Street. The next day I put in a tender for seventy dollars and got the job!

I gave notice to finish up as Topman at the wharf and also gave notice driving for Wimpy. Within a week I had become Port Hedland's new Rubbish Man.

Council's rubbish truck was a green painted Bedford J series tipper with a four cylinder diesel motor; the body

100

had openings in each side for loading and big swing doors at the back for dumping. The rubbish dump was located about one and a half kilometers out of town and had, at one time, been the Aboes' reserve.

Bedford Tipper Rubbish Truck

Unfortunately, most people in Port Hedland had never heard of dustbins; they all used forty four gallon steel drums. As the previous pickup service had been unreliable, a lot of people lit their bins and burnt their own rubbish; often the embers were still glowing red when I arrived to empty them. It was a common sight to see the whole truck alight, flames streaming out of its sides and running flat-out, heading for the dump! I can tell you now, there were some anxious moments. I realised just how physically fit I must have been, at the time, to cope with this type of work. Each full drum had to be lifted up over my shoulders and then tipped and shaken to dump out its contents into the truck—I probably lifted hundreds of them every day.

With the help of Council we eventually got the townsfolk to buy proper bins, for rubbish. When people got used to the regular, reliable service that I provided, the need to burn their rubbish disappeared and they were willing to let go of the old rusty drums. They knew I would be there, even on Christmas Day. There were no holidays as the job had to be done and being a one man show, it was difficult to catch up if I let the service lag.

Today is a public holiday and Dad is taking me with him on the rubbish truck. I had to get up really early when it was dark and he drove us around picking up the bins. I've been picking up the rubbish that has been spilled on the ground, or that the crows or dogs have managed to get out. Some bins have a wooden top with a brick on it so the rubbish is safe. When all the rubbish is inside, Dad lifts the bin up into the truck and empties it. Then we go on to the next one. Bins and rubbish are very smelly, but Dad says you get used to it.

The sun is coming up and we are driving out to the dump, to empty the truck. He pulls over to the side of the road and then I go and sit on his lap. We take off again and he works the gears and I'm on the big steering wheel. I have to reach right over to grab it and he helps me steer. It's good sitting up in the truck.

We're at the dump and Dad backs the truck up to a rubbish pile; we get out and he unlocks the back doors, swings them right around and fastens them to the sides. Now it's my turn and I get in the cab and flick the special switch to tip up the rubbish. I rev up the motor and up it goes; as the tipper gets higher, the rubbish starts to slide down. Dad shows me how to put the truck in first gear, quick change into second so we can jerk the last bit of rubbish out of the back. I can do first gear but keep missing second and stall the engine; so he comes and finishes off. We have a drink of water and then drive back into town to get some more. I hope I get to try second gear again.

Doing this job brought me in much closer contact with the Aboes and where they lived, as I would pick up their rubbish too. One of my least favourite sites was the reserve; the bins were often full of kangaroo or sheep's heads, bloody entrails, claws and fur, all crawling with maggots and guarded by swarms of biting flies.

On the reserve the Aboes lived in small green painted metal sheds set upon concrete slabs. These were single room buildings, which contained a cooker, sink and beds. The cookers were rarely used as they preferred to cook on an open fire and often dragged the beds outside to sleep where it was cooler. There was a community-use toilet block where the wall sheeting stopped about two hundred millimetres up from the slab; this was designed so the building could simply be hosed out, for cleaning.

Often a dead kangaroo or other animal carcass was hung up, outside on one of the tin hut's walls; when food was required they would slice off some meat and then go and hold it over one of the open fires until cooked. A course bread; damper was made with flour and water, balled up and then pushed into the embers of the fire to bake. When the bread was ready, they would break off the blackened crust and eat the soft interior. Most had a flagon of wine and were often drunk, especially if it was payday.

I got to know several of the Aboes and would often stay for a while to chat with one of the men, who rode an old Triumph motorbike. His father, who was quite elderly, sometimes joined us; the old man kept his door key pinned to the front of his singlet so he knew where it was. At other times a family would come to say hello and I'd meet their sometimes shy but always inquisitive children. They were a strong, wiry people and when they spoke their own language it was fast and at times, seemed very dramatic. Generally, their skin was quite dark and they had broad noses and wild curly hair; the men could look quite ferocious when they chose to.

One morning, one of the men came out with a badly swollen eye and a gash to the side of his head. I asked my mate what had happened. He explained that this man had gotten drunk in town and then come home and beaten his woman. The woman waited patiently until her drunken husband had fallen asleep outside near the fire, and then dropped a large rock on his head. He told me that the women get even when they are mistreated. I certainly saw a different side of Australia, emptying bins at the Aboriginal Reserve.

I started the rubbish run early in the morning and was generally finished by lunch time. I would go home and clean up to eat lunch with Molly. We would talk about the new house and what it would be like. We wanted three good sized bedrooms and a separate bathroom, toilet and laundry; and a big lounge with lots of light coming in. Molly suggested we begin by planting two Poinciana trees in the front yard, which would grow and shade the garden, and I had a novel idea for the verandah and fences. We wanted to make a bit of a statement in Port Hedland and a new house gave us lots of opportunities.

It was time to make some plans.

Grand Designs

Another First

Molly and I looked through a variety of house designs that we had found in magazines sent up from Perth. We planned a three bedroom layout with big wrap around verandahs on two sides. As part of my training to become an Aircraft Engineer I had prepared complex, scaled machinery drawing and so I drew up some house plans and elevations, then submitted them to Council.

I posted a copy of the plans down to a building supply company in Perth; they took off the quantities and quoted seven thousand dollars to supply and ship the building materials to Port Hedland. Within a few weeks the house plans were approved for building, and with our plans and approval in hand we met with the local Commonwealth Bank Manager, who agreed to loan us the money to build it. When the money came through, I contacted the building suppliers and gave them the job; the materials were to be delivered by cargo ship, which would take about a month.

The house would have three bedrooms and their walls were to be panels of full-height metal louvres, which would allow air to flow through the house during the hot summers. We were going to have the first sliding glass doors in Port Hedland; these would lead out onto a verandah that wrapped around the house on both street frontages. The verandah was quite deep and roofed to give shade and protection from the elements.

The kitchen was to be equipped with a gas stove, electric refrigerator and hot water. Most of Port Hedland's houses had a wood-chip water heater in the bathroom. People had to find small pieces of wood, pack the firebox and then light it. This was always messy and stunk the house out, not to mention waiting for the water to heat up. I opted for electric heating and a water storage tank, which proved to be a Godsend.

Port Hedland's water supply came from a bore sunk in the Turner River, forty kilometres southwest of the town. By the mid-sixties, supply was insufficient and new bores were sunk in the Yule River, some down to fifty metres, accessing a natural alluvial aquifer. For most of the year the two hundred kilometer long, ephemeral Yule was mostly dry, running only in the wet season and not every wet season. Water from both rivers was pumped through above-ground metal pipes, to reach consumers in the town.

During the summer months the water in the supply pipes got so hot that people couldn't shower until late at the night, when it had cooled sufficiently and they weren't going to get scalded. With our electric system and storage tank, the water cooled inside the house and provided us with relatively low temperature water to mix with the hot, when we needed it.

I realised that we were going to need a car. We had been getting around on bicycles and walking, or using the truck. I found a Holden FX sedan for sale and went to see it. The owner told me all about the great motor it

107

had; when I asked him to tell me, honestly, what was wrong with it he hesitated, nodded to himself and then lifted the floor mats. I looked inside and could see the roadway through the holes; it was rusted through. I bought the car for one hundred and fifty dollars and paid him for his honesty. It was blue-grey, had a six cylinder motor and four doors, so we could all fit in comfortably—just don't jump on the floor! I ended up screwing some plywood sheets across the floor pan and it worked great.

Mum and Dad drove Karen and I out to the block today in the FX. They had a big paper with the house drawing on it. We put stones down on the ground and scratched lines in the dirt for all the rooms. Dad had a big tape measure to get the sizes right. When the rocks were all down and the lines done, I went and stood in my bedroom and Karen in hers; Mum was in the kitchen and walked around her lounge room; Dad even pretended he was lying in a chair on the verandah, having a snooze.

Mum showed us where she had planted two Poinciana trees out the front, so they can begin growing, and a grass lawn will be there too. The trees have car tyres around them to keep the water in and protect them while they are little. Karen ran right around the house and then came in the back door. Ha-ha! Everyone is excited and laughing.

I'd taken Molly and the children out to the block to layout the house. They were both with Molly watering the new trees and I found myself alone at the fence-line looking over the property. For the first time since we'd arrived here I had a sense that we were going to be all right; that somehow this was really working. The house would be built and we would all have a home that was ours; not rented, not borrowed, but ours. In just fourteen months we had plenty of work, two blocks of land and a were designing our very first house. My mind opened up and I wondered what else I could do in Australia?

With our house, we were introducing new ideas into the town and people, who had been distant before, became more interested in us and asked about what we were up to next, how had so-and-so worked out and where did we get such-and-such from? And we were no longer the outsiders that we had been a year and a half ago, when we all slept on the wooden floor of a friend's house and I drove a taxi for twenty five pounds a week.

Albeit hot, dry and remote, Port Hedland was beginning to work for us and it was a welcome change.

Extending the Run

A Growing Business

The Shire Clerk called me in to say that Council were installing new public rubbish bins around the town and they would need emptying three times a week, including one at Pretty Pool. We negotiated a new contract rate for the extended run and my business grew.

Pretty Pool is one of my favourite places in Port Hedland. It's east from our place about six kilometers out; too far to walk so we have to wait for Dad to take us there.

When the tide goes out it leaves a swimming hole, and back up the creek a little there are oyster beds with crabs and little fish. When we go on the oysters, we have to watch our for stone fish and wear shoes or thongs. The school kids told me to watch out as sometimes a shark or crocodile might be left in the swimming hole when the tide goes out, but I haven't seen any. Even so, when we get there we have a good look in the water before we get in for a swim; it's clear and we can see the bottom. There's the sandy beach and over the water on the other side of the pool is a rocky ledge. All of us kids climb up there and then jump off into the water; bomb dives are good.

Out on the sand bar, when the tide is running out, I find lots of shells; cowrie shells and they are really nice, some are as big as my hand. I have to sneak up on them or they dig into the sand really quick and disappear. The sand bar is big and I can walk a long way out. When the tide is in we fish here; up near the mangroves is good and around the rocks, but we mainly come out to swim.

On the beach is one rubbish bin and a shelter, which is good when it's really hot.

Council was also interested in me taking over the job of emptying septic tanks in the area. Houses in Port Hedland had an in-ground septic system. All waste went into a concrete holding tank containing two chambers; when bacteria had broken down the solids in one, liquid would drain out of the tank into trenches and either soak away in the soil or evaporate. In the tank, a crust formed on top of the liquid creating a sealed environment, and if it became too thick the system wouldn't operate properly. Council maintained the tanks by pumping them out from time to time. Septic systems, generally, worked very well and were virtually odourless; in fact, later on I top-dressed my front lawn with some of the crust!

The clerk said Council had an old tractor, a trailer with a holding tank onboard and a mud pump to use for the extraction. I quoted fifteen dollars per house for my labour and they would supply and maintain the equipment. I was very happy with the extra income as it would help us pay for the new house.

Stephen Outram

In The Trenches

Making Foundations

In the summer of 1966 I borrowed a builder's dumpy
level, set out the house on-site and began digging
trenches for the footings. The block and surrounding
area had fared surprisingly well after Tropical Cyclone
Shirley's earlier visit in April, and Lisa and Betty who
came before her. This gave me confidence that we
would not be washed out during future rainy seasons,
as Shirley had been a powerful Category 3 cyclone that
had drenched the town and caused widespread flooding.

The soil was dry and mainly sand, and the trenches
tended to cave-in as they were dug; as I removed
material, I had to install timber shuttering along the
trenches to hold up the sides. The block had a wide
shallow hump and I shovelled this, by hand, into the
centre of the house to act as fill for the slab, which
would be finished three hundred millimeters above
ground level. L-shaped reinforcing bars were tied in
place to connect the slab later, and using a cement
mixer, wheelbarrow and shovel I poured the footings
all in one day. Several weeks later I broke away the
formwork and was very happy to see a ring beam; a
rectangle of solid concrete with the steel bars poking up
like soldiers all in a row.

I got to work filling and leveling the area that the slab

would sit on and built the shuttering for that. When
it was ready—with the help of Molly, Stephen, Karen
and some friends—we mixed cement in a petrol driven
mixer, hauled it in a wheelbarrow and poured the slab.
As each barrow of cement was slopped in place, we used
long widths of timber to tamp it down and smooth
the surface. When it began to harden I covered the
green concrete over with plastic sheets, pieces of carpet,
linoleum and anything I could find. That evening I set
several water sprinklers running, to keep the slab from
drying-out too quickly in the intense summer heat and
cracking. I went home, cleaned up and fell into bed,
exhausted; I had to be up early the next morning to
collect rubbish.

The next day, during the rubbish run, I dropped by
Brearley Street to check on the slab. I was furious to
find that someone had turned off the sprinklers and
quickly got them running water again. Fortunately
the slab survived; If it had cracked, I would've had to
bulldoze the whole thing and then start all over again.

I remembered my hard work collecting the cement
sweepings from various cargo ship's holds—when the
last wheelbarrow of concrete had been dumped and
the house slab was fully poured, we'd opened just two
additional bags of shop-bought cement to finish off; a
huge saving!

Move Number 4

A Turning Point

After the summer rains, we decided to check the wooden crates we had shipped from England, which contained most of our worldly goods and chattels. Up until now there had been nowhere to unpack anything and the crates had followed us around and ended up on the hard-standing at the back of Wimpy's. Unfortunately, the crates had been penetrated by the season's heavy rains. It was a mistake on our part to have left them out; they were never designed for Port Hedland's powerful weather. Family photographs, clothes, blankets, books, documents and papers were damp, mildewed and ruined; our wedding photographs and other memorabilia were lost too and we had to shed most of our gear.

This was a big blow for both of us, especially for Molly who was looking forward to enjoying some of her precious things. It seemed to be a tipping point for her and she decided she'd had enough of Port Hedland. One night Molly broke down and cried, and told me she wanted to return to Perth. I could see my wife was desperately unhappy; apart from the heat, cyclones, cramped living quarters, minimal facilities and the fact that we were "off the boat poms" in a small Australian outback town, I suspected that Wimpy had been trying to get her into his bed. With me having been away so much working, it had been an additional and unbearable pressure on Molly.

I put all of our ruined gear back into their crates, borrowed one of Wimpy's trucks and took them out to the rubbish dump. All of those ruined things that had been part of our lives, the many items that were so familiar and comforting, I threw them all into a smoldering pile. It exposed a nerve and as I watched them burn I began to doubt myself and questioned what I was doing here. Was this really what I wanted for my family and myself? Maybe Port Hedland was a mistake and I should look for aircraft work in Sydney or Melbourne as we had originally planned. A few days later I started looking for a truck that would be returning to Perth and could transport our gear south, and then fate stepped in and gave us a second choice.

The Department of Housing contacted us and we were offered a commission house. It was a game changer for both of us and we accepted.

The house was located at 63 Morgan Street, not far from the Wiles' place. A family of Aboes had it before us and it took us some time to clean it up. They had used the cooker as an open fireplace, I can remember using a hammer and chisel on the inside of the toilet to get it clean and the yard was overgrown with metre high grass! It was a basic three bedroom place with a hardwood timber floor and small verandah on the front; all up on stumps with external louvres over the windows. It had a pipe framed fence with chicken wire infill and a Hills Hoist clothes line out the back. It turned out that Robbie's ship was in port for the weekend; he and a couple of mates, armed with a carton

115

of beer, helped us paint it out.

When it was all done and ready for us, Molly and I packed up all of our belongings at Wimpy's and moved in. It was our fourth move and finally, we had our very own house! We had a bedroom, the kids had their bedrooms and life began to get brighter.

I'm lying in my bed, in my bedroom, in our house. Nobody else lives here but the Outrams. The floor is wooden and the walls are all clean and white. There are different rooms: a kitchen for the cooking, a lounge for sitting and eating, everyone has a bedroom, I don't have to go outside to use the bathroom and Mum is much happier. Having your own home is good.

A sheep is outside in the yard, eating all the grass. We're not friends yet; he runs away. I can catch him but he doesn't like it. I went under the house today; it's all red dirt and stumps. There are metal caps on the stumps to stop the ants getting up into the house, and some spiders with red spots. I don't touch them. I can see the beams and hear the others walking around inside; the floor boards squeak a bit.

I went out the back and climbed up on the clothes line and then swung around, until Mum yelled at me to get off. Karen can hide in the tall grass and we play hide and seek. Tonight we sat in the lounge and played Gin Rummy cards, then I had to go to bed. Karen goes before me because she is younger. I would like to stay up later.

There are louvres across my window, on the outside, but I can see out to the street when I look through the side. I like my room. Mum and Dad are on the verandah talking quietly; I smell their cigarettes. A car drives past. I can hear the crickets and the house creaks a little.

Our new neighbours were Ray and Margaret Ford. They had two girls and turned out to be a nice family. Ray was a mechanic, working for Mt. Goldsworthy and Margaret cleaned houses.

Molly set up her hairdressing in the lounge room and we settled in to resume our life in Port Hedland. I even managed to rent a sheep from one of the local stations for a month, who did a great job of mowing the grass and giving us access to the yard. I bought bicycles for everyone, from Perth, and it was very exciting for the kids when they arrived. There were a few spills as they learned to ride, particularly with Stephen who discovered jumping, skidding and the joys of gravel rash.

I'm riding my bike really fast along the road side and the front wheel hits a pot hole. Suddenly the handlebars spin in my hands and the wheel jams; I'm catapulted off the bike. I get my hands out front but land on my chest in the gravel and slide along. I hear the bike crash behind me and we both come to a halt with dust everywhere.

My hands hurt, my chest hurts even more and my knees are sore. Ouch! I get up off the road, pick up my bike and walk it home. Mum is there and she just shakes her head. We go into the bathroom and she cleans the scratches, then puts on iodine with a cotton stick. Ouch; that really stings and it turns my skin yellow. She tells me that she can't put plasters on

117

gravel rash and I have to go sit on the verandah and let the iodine dry; and to stay home now.

I have a comic on the verandah. Mum cleans up in the bathroom and I go outside to sit on the verandah steps. Goodness, everything hurts now. My bike is leaning against the fence; it's got some scratches and the handlebars are twisted around the wrong way. I hope Dad can fix it for me.

Candy

A Blonde Arrives

One day, after we had been in the Morgan Street house several months, a beautiful and unexpected thing happened. A customer, while ringing up for a hairdressing appointment, asked if we wanted a puppy; a Labrador. When this beautiful bundle of blonde fluff arrived nobody, especially me, could refuse and Karen named the little female Candy. So, we had another member of the family and she fitted in beautifully

Candy is so soft. Karen just cuddles her all the time. But she wiggles away; she likes to play or fall asleep under one of the beds. Her teeth are little but really sharp, like needles. She doesn't bite that hard. And she likes to chew Dad's boots; actually, she chews everything. I like her. When I run around the house she chases me barking. She can't catch me now, but maybe soon when she grows. She makes us all laugh. Good thing the sheep is gone; I'm not sure how they would get on. We keep the gate closed so she doesn't run out into the road; she likes to explore everywhere, and sniff everything. We love her!

As Candy grew up I trained her, and every day she rode in the rubbish truck with me; she became very well known amongst the town folk as she got to visit every house and business in the area. We spent a lot of time together and formed a strong bond; most of the time she knew what I was thinking long before I said anything. And while she adored the whole family, she was my dog and she new it, and I was her man and I knew it. It's funny how an animal can get under your skin, in the way that Candy did with me.

Greens or Browns?

Golf in the Bush

It was no surprise to me that Port Hedland didn't have
a golf course, but I began to think about it. I had played
golf in England and loved the game. I asked around to
see if there was any interest in golf and a golf course;
there was. A group of us talked with Council and they
agreed to let us have some land out near the race track,
for a course, and we could use their slasher.

It was too hot to play in summer so we began planning
a seven hole layout to be ready for the winter months.
I borrowed Council's tractor-slasher and took Stephen
with me to cut the first fairways. The site was basic—
natural sandy scrubland with few features—but it was
large enough for a couple of decent par five holes and
several shorter ones.

Dad and I are roaring around on the tractor making a
golf course. We are cutting around some bushes and
then making long runs up and down, up and down.
There's dust, rocks and sticks going everywhere,
blasting out of the slasher, and we are making
roadways in the sand. I would like to drive the tractor
but Dad says the steering is too heavy for me so I'm
riding shotgun. Wahoo!

After the fairways were cut a group of us walked them

121

and threw rocks, branches and other debris off to the side; and marked the larger items to be picked up by truck later on. Forty four gallon drums were collected, painted white and placed along the edges of each fairway; this would help us actually see the fairways as they were the same sandy colour as the rough. In addition, the drums would help by providing a line-of-sight for determining the out of bounds rules. We also managed to get enough old railway sleepers to use for tees. Four sleepers were placed together on the ground forming a box and then filled with dirt; they were heavy hardwood timbers and once the dirt had baked in the sun, it all held together fairly well. Then we made the greens, but the greens were not really green.

Port Hedland's greens should have really been called browns as they were made up of oiled sand. Clean sand was dumped onto the ground and raked out into a rough circle and then the oil sprinkled on top. The oil soaked in and caused the grains of sand to stick together. Over time the oil evaporated and needed to be reapplied, so we collected used oil from trucks and other machinery at service time and saved it in drums. It was quite pungent and we joked that a blind golfer could at least smell their way to the green!

To putt, the idea was that a golfer picked up their ball off the green and placed it to one side, while they smoothed a path to the hole. This was done with a bar, which was a simple flat steel bar welded to a handle—towards the end of winter, these bars were so hot from the heat of the sun that it was difficult to hold onto them for long. The bar was dragged across the oiled sand, to level-out a suitable putting surface and then the ball was replaced ready to putt. Putting on sand was an art as the ball picked up grit as it rolled, and golf shoes were never the same after a few games as they soaked up the oil.

A length of twisted steel reinforcing rod, with red cloth that Molly sewed, was used for the flag; this leaned out of a piece of tube steel that had been hammered into the ground and served as the hole.

The fairways were largely dirt with tufts of hardy bush-grass. There were small rocks and stones to be dealt with and every player's clubs were chipped along the leading edge. In addition to the stones, some locals regularly smashed beer bottles in certain areas and this made for an interesting and unusual hazard, as players had to negotiate these crunchy mine fields that sparkled brightly in the sun.

Another unusual characteristic of the course was that it had to be rebuilt each season. During the eight metre high King Tides, which occurred twice each year, the low-land course disappeared underwater. The tees, literally, floated away and our greens were washed out. So, each season we went and found all of the timber sleepers and white drums, and put them back in place, slashed the fairways, removed any obstacles that had showed up and built new greens.

The club house was a metal shed containing some chairs and an old kerosene refrigerator—this had been scrounged from an abandoned caravan, fixed, and put to good use. We would light up the fridge at the start of a game and fill it with beer and drinks; by the time we had finished the bottles were nicely cooled.

After a round of golf in the sun, the fridge and its chilled bottles were the only thing on anyone's mind. Players kept score on scrap pieces of paper and we had a blackboard on the wall to tally up the winners and runners-up for each game. It all seemed to work quite well.

On the way home from school I often visit Mrs. Whitty; she's like a Grandmother and always has really nice biscuits and cakes. Her husband died and she lives in the house alone. We are friends. I'm telling her about how my Dad is playing golf and I would like to play too. She says that she might have something for me and we are going down the side of her house and in underneath. She's found some golf clubs; two bamboo shafted irons and a putter. She says they were her husband's and gives them to me. I am very happy; my own golf clubs. Wow!

It's Sunday. Jimmy and I are waiting behind the tin clubhouse until the last group of men have hit off, then we are playing. We don't have any golf balls yet so we play with stones; there's plenty to choose from. We have done two holes and now we've found a lost golf ball. Wow! It goes really far and I hit it into the bush; we are off running to find it. Jimmy finds the ball and we are back on the fairway again. We get the ball to the sand and rake it just like the men do. Jimmy has the first putt, then me and it's in the hole. We jump around and cheer. Hooray!

I noticed that Stephen had begun playing on the course with a friend; they were following on after the main field had played through. He had managed to get himself a couple of clubs and the two of them seemed to be having a good time with our lost golf balls. I gave him several of my old golf balls, some tees and made sure we had soft drinks in the clubhouse refrigerator for them when they came in. Stephen learned about the infamous nineteenth hole and I taught him a little about the game, par and how to score. Maybe he might go on to be another Arnold Palmer or Jack Nicklaus?

Stephen Outram

Hardwood Framed

Walls and a Roof

With the concrete slab down and curing, I started building the wall frames using a one hundred by seventy five millimetre hardwood section. The main frames were cut, assembled and nailed together on the slab, then stacked over on one side ready to be erected later. It turned out that the slab was not perfectly level so a series of timber chocks were placed around the perimeter to create a level base for the wall panels.

I'm passing Dad the nails that he's using to make the walls. They are seventy five millimetres long, and look like little shiny spears. He has to hit the nails really hard with his hammer to drive them through the hard wood studs. Sometimes they bend and he bangs them straight again. When I have a go I can hardly get them to stick in the wood and sometimes I miss the nail altogether! He says I better go and practice on some scrap wood until I get my eye in and gives me his spare hammer. I get some nails and wood, and take it all into my bedroom.

The floor is all covered with sand; Dad says that the sand will protect the concrete from the hot sun while it gets really hard. I put the point end to the wood and hold the nail like my Dad does, then I swing the hammer down but it jumps off and gets my thumb.

126

Ouch! It stings and I shake my hand. Dad comes over and shows me how to let the hammer do the work; rather than forcing it to hit the nail, just guide it onto the nail. That's better. I hit it!

Once all the main wall panels were ready, I got in some help to stand and fix them in position; being hardwood, they were quite heavy and cumbersome to lift. With the frames firmly braced, all of the roof's beams and rafters were lifted up, positioned and fixed to the top of the walls. In just a few days the house changed dramatically as it stood up in the air and its size and volume became apparent. It was exciting to drive along Anderson Street and, from a distance, actually see the building. I took Molly and the kids out to see it and we were able to walk through openings and explore our future rooms.

With Port Hedland being an area that experiences a large number of tropical cyclones every year, plenty of galvanized metal framing plates were used to make sure that the roof stayed attached to the walls and they to the floor slab. Towards the end of 1966 all of the framing was in place and I worked on to have the house watertight before 1967's rainy season set in. Fitting the roof sheeting, flashing and gutters was a specialist's job and I got a local contractor in to handle that part of the build.

When he was done I got busy cladding the external walls, fitting windows and getting ready for the rain.

Stephen's Volcano

A Close Call

While we were living in the UK, Stephen got interested in fire. At one point, while we were living in a caravan park in Brandon, Surrey it had become very dangerous. He stole paraffin from several caravans and used it to light a fire, deep within a large woodpile; the woodpile was located near the park's gas bottle storage shed and the fire brigade had to be called to put it out. We were nearly thrown out of the park for that one!

I never told Mum and Dad about another fire, the haystack that I set alight. It was in a field next to the caravan park. A friend and I had made a small tunnel in the hay and were flicking lit matches into it and then putting out the flames before the hay caught alight; it was going really well, except for the last match we flicked.

When we realised that we couldn't extinguish the flames we ran and hid in the playground next door. Over the trees we could see flames and smoke pouring out of it, then the fire brigade came, sirens wailing. They put the fire out and left a pile of black ash on the ground. It was a good thing I was only caught for the woodpile one. Oops!

One afternoon, after finishing the rubbish run, I drove

home and parked the truck outside. I walked up to
the house and smelled smoke, but couldn't see where
it was coming from. I ran up the steps into the house
but everything seemed normal inside. I went out to the
front again and bent down to look under the house.

The boys at school told me about 'volcanos,' and
I'm making my own in the dirt under the house. I've
scooped out a shallow depression and laid in several
sheets of newspaper. Now I'm putting a lit match in
the centre and the paper has caught alight. Before
it burns too much I lay another sheet of newspaper
on top, let it just burn through and then another
and another and another. It really looks like a
smouldering volcano. Wow!

Dad's just yelled at me; my heart jumped. What's up
Dad? He's got my leg and is dragging me out from
under the house. I'm out and he tells me not to
move or I'm dead. Dad's really mad. Now he's under
the house, putting out my volcano! Do I run and
hide or do I stay? I stay and start crying as hard and as
loud as I can.

I pulled Stephen out, then scrambled under the house
and threw dirt over the burning newspapers. I was
furious; what was he doing lighting fires under a timber
house, or any house! I got out and he was still there,
crying. I told him I would give him something to cry
about and held onto his arm while I spanked him with
my other hand. He tried to run and we ended up going
around and around in circles, until I was done.

I didn't like spanking my kids but his stupidity in
lighting the fire could have cost us our house and all

of our gear. I told him to go to his room and stay there until I called him for dinner and let go of his arm. He ran off crying, tears streaking his dusty cheeks.

I sat down on the steps for a while and calmed myself down; my hands were shaking. After a while I got up and went and made some bricks in the driveway; it felt better to concentrate on something else and hopefully, Molly would be home soon. Stephen cried for a long time.

I'm sitting on the floor in the corner of my room. Mum is home but she doesn't come in. I can hear them talking. I smell their cigarette smoke. I hear noises in the kitchen; she's making dinner and later she comes to get me. Mum sits on my bed and talks quietly to me about lighting fires; about setting the house alight and that we'd have nowhere to live. I tell her that I just wanted to build a volcano and see what it was like, but I can see that under the house was not the place to do it. I tell her I'm sorry and we go to have dinner. Dad doesn't say much and he doesn't look at me; it's like we are not friends anymore. I won't light any more fires; I promise.

Hand Made

Five Hundred Bricks

With the building work I was doing I needed a different car; the sedan was not really suitable and so I sold it and bought a Standard Vanguard ute. It had an impressive "roo" bar on the front and the rear tray was covered. Its paint was terrible and I hand-painted the body lemon-yellow; it sure stood out!

Candy liked the new car and would ride around balancing on the tailgate. And we even slept in it while attending a weekend gymkhana out in the bush. It certainly made my life easier carting gear out to Brearley Street.

I had a bright idea about fancy bricks around the house, when I saw a red steel mould advertised in a building magazine. It would make a three hundred by three hundred by one hundred millimetre concrete brick with decorative holes. I ordered the tool and it was sent up from Perth.

Along the side of our current house I set up four lengths of steel tube spanning across a couple of wooden stands, a work bench, sand pile and bags of cement—Candy and the neighbour's black dog enjoyed the sand pile; it was cool and much softer than sun baked ground of our yard. I also cut sixteen squares out of asbestos-cement sheeting; these would sit across two of the tubes.

Every afternoon, for about a month, I assembled the mould on top of a square sheet. I had mixed up a weak mixture—one of cement to four of sand—and pounded it into the mould with a wooden tool.  When it was firm, the mould was broken down revealing a perfect green brick, which I carefully lifted onto the steel tubes to dry and harden. By the time Molly called us for dinner, there were two rows of eight bricks lined up side by side. The next day I stacked the sixteen bricks in a pile up against the house and began the process again.

The dogs, Karen and I all like to sit on the sand pile and hang around with Dad when he's making bricks. The neighbour's dog is black with white paws. He is friends with Candy, especially when she is on-heat! We have to keep all the gates closed then and he stays outside, or Mum says there will be black and yellow striped puppies to look after.

Dad is often working on the bricks when I get home from school. He likes making things and is happy each time a new brick comes out of the mould, to go on the tubes. It seems similar to when Mum makes a cake or a roast dinner and takes it out of the oven; it makes them happy. It's different being with them when they are making things.

Eventually, I had made five hundred fancy bricks and would use them to fence the block and the house's verandah. In addition, I made another seventy two solid bricks to be gate posts at the driveway and entry.

Finishing Off

And a New Job

Brearley Street was moving closer to completion and
was now at lockup stage; Molly and I began to look at
how we would finish the interior and ordered catalogues
and brochures from various Perth building material
suppliers. We spent hours browsing through a growing
pile that was stacked in the corner of our lounge room.
In a flooring catalogue, I discovered a large format,
three hundred by three hundred millimetre, vinyl floor
tile. I chose a lovely blue tile with a subtle marbling
effect for the main floor areas and a patterned kitchen
tile featuring black and white strips, and placed an
order.

While I had been building our house, several other
homes had started nearby; the builders had come over,
interested in what I was doing, and I'd gotten to know
John who was constructing our neighbour's new house.
It was a good connection to make and he introduced
me to a plumber and electrician who I employed.

Working with John's plumber we got the kitchen,
laundry, bathroom and toilet fitted and then I cleaned
up the concrete floor ready to receive tiles, which had
been delivered along with several drums of adhesive and
some tools.

Before I glued any tiles down I did a dry run and laid out long runs of tiles to see how they would work in all of the rooms. There had to be a starting point and the first tile would determine the pattern throughout the whole house. I did a run along the hallway's centre-line and after half a day's experimentation, with different combinations, saw how it would work. I left the guide tiles in place and stacked boxes of blue tiles in all of the rooms ready to begin the next day, after I'd finished my rubbish run.

I laid the tiles, carefully cutting them in around corners, doorways, skirting boards and floor drains. It was very satisfying work and as each room was finished, and the drab, grey concrete replaced with lustrous blue, I took a long moment to enjoy what I'd created. This was very different work to the wharf or my rubbish run, where it had to be done over and over again; and even with the aircraft work that I had done in England there was a large element of maintenance. With tiling, I ended up with a seamless expanse of beautiful flooring that would be there tomorrow and every day after that. It's funny, but laying the floor in my own house changed me as I became aware that I could do more than just maintain, I could make a finished product. To me, it was like art!

When the floor was done, John came over to see what I'd been up to. He took one look and asked me if I would do all of his houses. I said that I would and was off with another job; we agreed a price of one dollar and fifty cents per square metre to lay the tiles and he would provide all of the materials. I was to begin as soon as my own house was done.

Black Tie

Undertaking, a New Job?

The Shire Council telephoned and requested I consider becoming Port Hedland's Undertaker. For a moment, I was speechless; perhaps a little shocked and my mind raced over to the old cemetery that was just a short distance from Brearley Street and the new house we were building. Its sun-bleached headstones stood out starkly across the sparse landscape and we walked along its eastern boundary on our way to the beach.

At one time it had been known as the Pioneer and Pearlers Cemetery but, more recently, it was called the Old Port Hedland Cemetery. It had been located on the corner of Sutherland and Stevens Streets since 1912. The land held the remains of over five hundred people, divided into distinct sections: Roman Catholic, Protestant, Aboriginal and Asian. Generally, it looked worn and was overgrown with weeds and grasses; some of the grave plots were difficult to see and some had sustained damage, probably due to slashing.

After I recovered from the shock, I asked what this Undertaker's job entailed. Ian Rogers, the Shire Clerk, described that there was an Aboe who would dig the hole at the cemetery and then fill it in afterwards; he was paid three dollars. Council had a flatbed Volkswagon to use as a hearse and kept a supply of coffins. I was required to coordinate the hole's location, the Aboe, a priest and the grieving family. I would pick up a coffin and then drive to the hospital, where the body would be released to me. The corpse had to be lifted into the coffin and if rigor mortis had set in, then I would straighten the limbs and push them down so the lid could be screwed on. Handles were fixed to the coffin's sides and it was slid up onto the hearse and secured.

I had to put on a black tie and then drive slowly to the Sutherland Street cemetery, where the priest and family would, hopefully, be waiting. After the priest had finished his service, the Aboe and I would lower the coffin into its hole and then he would fill the hole in. Finally, I would complete the appropriate documents and post them off to the Registrar of Deaths in Perth.

Being hungry for money, my second question was about the pay. Ian told me that I would get twenty dollars for an adult and twelve dollars for a child, black or white. The whole conversation was quite bizarre and I told him I would think about it.

I talked this over with Molly who laughed out loud and told me that I couldn't do it; I was just not the type to be an Undertaker. Of course she was right; the idea of handling a corpse put me right off. I rang Ian, declined his unusual offer and Council looked elsewhere. I'm sure he chuckled to himself when he put the phone down.

Stephen Outram

Holidays

Cottesloe and the Manly Hostel

We had been working hard in Port Hedland for over two years now and were both getting tired; I decided to set up a family holiday in Perth. Robbie, our friendly steward, was given the job of finding us some accommodation.

I needed someone to take-on the rubbish run for a few weeks and began to look for someone in a similar situation. I talked with Ken Nichols, a local haulage contractor I knew who sold sand and gravel in the area. He told me that he would like to take holidays too and we agreed to help each other out. Ken would look after Port Hedland's rubbish while I was away in Perth with the family, and I would run his gravel trucks for him. Ken was to take his holiday first, in March. His timing was good as he missed Tropical Cyclone Gwen; I didn't.

Molly had a hairdresser who could cope with the salon, and they arranged to reduce the number of bookings while we were away to make it easier for her. Our new house was ready to be finished inside and I lined up a painter to do the work while we were away. It all looked good!

Unfortunately for me, everyone wanted sand and gravel while Ken was away. I was getting up at four o'clock in the morning and working the rubbish run until two in the afternoon, and then driving Ken's trucks until dark. On top of that, Gwen crossed the coast near Broome and caused massive local flooding, she even managed to bring down one of Port Hedland's huge fresh water storage tanks and washed out railway lines; it was not much fun to work in. When the time came to get onboard Robbie's ship and sail for Perth, I collapsed and slept for two days straight.

The ship has stopped at Onslow. The town used to have a really long jetty but it was damaged during cyclones. Our ship is unloading horses onto a barge, tied up alongside. The horses are in big wooden crates, which are lifted by the ship's winches out of the hold and then lowered over the side down onto the barge. The horses seem quite okay with being out at sea and flying through the air.

Robbie had found a hostel for us right opposite Cottesloe Beach, which was just perfect. Molly and I had a bedroom and the kids slept on the verandah outside our window. It was full board, including three meals a day in the dining room, and accommodation. Everything was within walking distance: the beach, shops, there was a golf course just up the road and a picture theatre nearby. Perfect for all of us!

Manly Hostel was built in Cottesloe by Councillor, George Henry West in 1908. It was located on the corner of Swanbourne Terrace[1] and John Street and looked out, directly west, over Cottesloe Beach and the Indian Ocean. It was an impressive two story building

---

1   Later renamed to Marine Parade.

that was dominated by large wide verandas on both street fronts and featured lattice panels, shallow arched decorative beams and posts. Originally, it offered forty rooms but was extended in later years.

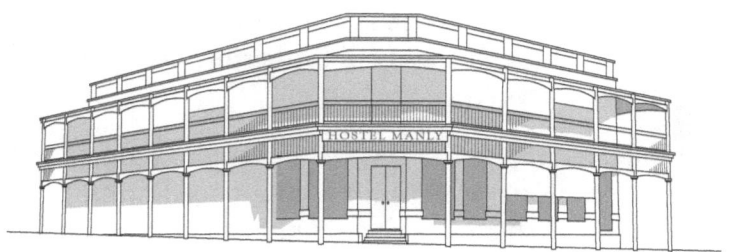

Manly Hostel, Cottesloe Beach

Our room looks out between the bathing pavilion and a big tall pine tree; we see the ocean every day and hear the waves at night. Out in the ocean is a floating buoy; I'm going to swim out there one day. We can watch the sun set. My bed and Karen's bed is on the verandah; they both have grey blankets and never get wet because the roof over us is really wide.

At night time, the staff come around and pull down big shades to stop the early morning sun shining in on our beds; but we wake up early anyway. It's fun to climb in through the window to get in the room where Mum and Dad's bed is, then back out to our beds. There's a big bathroom down the hall from our room and we have to lock the door when we are in there, because other people use it too.

We were on the beach every day enjoying the water and lazing in the warm summer sun. We read books, talked, slept, rested, played with the kids and began to relax; I noticed that we all laughed a lot more too.

I'm exploring on the other side of the rock groyne, just down from the main beach. There's not much sand here, mainly rocks leading down to the water. I can see a white surfboard up on the rocks. It looks pretty good and there's no one around. It must have washed up. I'm a bit nervous in case someone should see me, but I'm picking it up and taking it over to show Mum and Dad. I tell Dad that I found it on the rocks and he seems okay with that. Phew! I thought he might tell me to take it back. It's foam and floats me easily; I paddle out past the surf and then get up on my knees. I see the buoy out there, bobbing in the swell; soon I will swim right around you.

Every afternoon Karen would go missing. One minute she was on the beach with us and the next we looked around and she was gone. I followed her one day and soon learned where she was going to. Karen had discovered something she had never seen before, television. There was no television or even radio in Port Hedland, so this was something completely novel and she was hooked. The hostel had a dedicated TV room and in the afternoons it was empty; most adults went in to watch the news and other shows in the early evening, so Karen could watch whatever she liked. Later in the afternoon Stephen would join her there until we called them out for dinner.

Lost in Space; I love that show and it's on every afternoon. Dr. Smith is funny and he's always getting in trouble. And the robot goes around waving his big arms yelling, "Danger! Danger!" or sometimes he plays the guitar. Will Robinson, he's pretty smart

141

but Dr. Smith tries to trick him into doing things he should not do. The Robinson family all live on a spaceship and fly around to different planets and galaxies. I would so like a spaceship, and a robot.

We caught up with the friends we'd made on Fairsky, Susanna and Peter, who were very unsettled in Perth. They were renting accommodation in the city and found work hard to get. Since settling in Port Hedland, we had kept in touch by letter and they told us they were seriously thinking of going to America, where they could continue their careers in dancing and music.

They had a car and took us for a drive one day, out to visit our block of land. Many of the big trees had been felled and there was a much more open space, but it was still largely undeveloped. We had already paid the loan out, so the land was ours. It was good to see it and walk the boundary. We drove back into Perth, bid our friends goodbye and wished them well in the United States. They left and Stephen and I managed to get a quick swim in, before dinner.

Dad and I are having a swim and I mention the buoy to him. He asks if I would like to swim out there. Yes please! We begin to swim out; I duck my head down and the water is clear below us. As we go further out it gets deeper and I can't see the bottom any more. We keep swimming and reach the buoy. We can't touch it because there's barnacles on the side; a big chain goes down into the water. The sun goes behind a cloud and the water gets really dark. I'm glad to see that Dad is swimming back and race in after him. I look back at the buoy; I told you I would get here.

142

We worked out the local busses and took the kids to see a circus in the city; and went to Beatty Park one day, a huge complex with several swimming pools and high diving boards that had been used for the 1962 British Empire and Commonwealth Games. We also visited London Court again and bought some familiar sweets and other English goodies. Along the Swan River we found a big windmill and a ship that was covered with lights and looked brilliant at night; and made a trip up to beautiful Kings Park overlooking the Narrows Bridge.

Molly bought herself the latest bikini, black with red flowers, to go with her super suntan, Stephen learned to surf with his new board and went fishing off the rock groyne, Karen explored television and we all thoroughly enjoyed our two weeks at Cottesloe Beach. But all too soon it was time to get on a State Ship and sail north, back to Port Hedland. In two days time I would be working on the bins and Molly cutting and perming someone's hair. There was no limit to the luggage we could carry on the ship, so we made sure we filled our bags with lots of goodies.

Down the back stairs of Manly Hostel is a store room, where people can put their beach chairs, flippers, masks and other beach stuff. Mum and Dad say that I can't take my surfboard back to Port Hedland so I'm hiding it in this room. I've got a good spot in the corner and have laid it down behind some chairs, with my red-striped beach towel over it. I'm going to go surfing again when we come back; it should be safe in here, until then.

When we got back to Port Hedland, the yellow ute was

143

waiting for us at the jetty. I had loaned it to a tiler while we were away and he had left it for us. We walked up to the car and saw that it was wrecked; the rear cover was broken, the tailgate hanging lose and its body scratched and damaged. I was furious!

The next morning I went to see the tiler and he sheepishly told me the story. His mate's truck had broken down some way out of town and they had taken the ute out to have a look. They couldn't fix the truck but had managed to jack it up high enough so that they could get one of its front wheels in the back of the ute, and rest the chassis across its rear guard. Then they drove my yellow ute back into town, with the truck loaded on it. He ended up giving me some money to go towards fixing the damage, but the Vanguard never recovered its former yellow glory.

The good news was that No 2 Brearley Street was painted; it was finished inside and so we all moved in. It was truly wonderful to be in our own home at last.

Move number five; done!

The Picture Gardens

Entertainment

In 1967 a drive-in cinema was built about one and a half kilometers out of town; up until then the picture gardens were our source of entertainment.

Port Hedland's Picture Gardens were located at number six Wedge Street and run by Joyce and Jack Glass. The gardens had been there since 1936 when they were built by Charles Bayman. The original screen was made of flat iron sheeting fixed to a timber frame; it and the six foot high perimeter fences had to be regularly repaired due to cyclone damage. In the late forties, Bayman built a concrete screen, which could withstand the summer weather.

A maximum of three hundred and fifty people could be accommodated sitting in canvas chairs or on the ground, and until the mid sixties screening was only on Saturday nights.

We are lining up at the ticket windows to get our entry ticket; Dad has the money so he is first. Now, we go to the main gate and get our tickets clipped so we can go in. The seats are in rows and made of striped canvas that hangs over lengths of water pipe; they are long seats that we all share. When someone gets up or sits down, it bumps all the other people on

145

the seat. Sometimes we kids bounce up and down on the seats, but the adults tell us to sit still. The lights are still on so I go and muck around with some of my friends. Kids can sit anywhere but the white people always sit at the back.

They are turning the garden lights out now and the big screen lights up. I sit next to Mum; she has some lollies and crisps. The film is playing and we can see geckos running across the screen, and bats sometimes fly across the projector light and cast shadows on the picture.

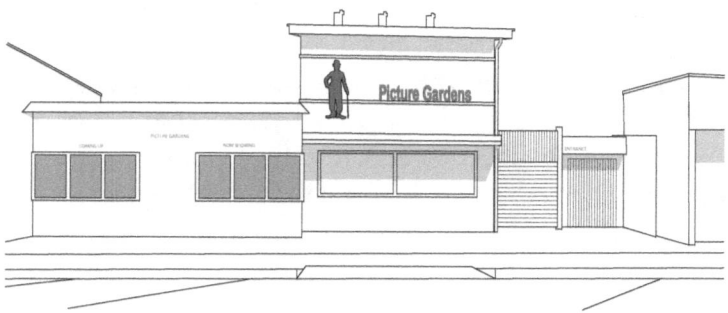

Port Hedland Picture Gardens

The seating was organised so that Aboes were down the front and whites sat at the back. We got two feature films each week on a Saturday night, and screening ran from seven thirty until midnight. Everybody went and the kids loved it. Occasionally, after the cinema had closed, the adults used to gather together in the town hall for a dance; we would bring our own music, drinks and food, and make up a party.

Mum is shaking me and I open my eyes. I'm looking up at the sky and can see a million stars. She tells me

146

that I fell asleep during the second film. It's time to go home and everyone is leaving. We go out of the gate and a lot of people are standing around talking and laughing; no one seems in a hurry to go home. Port Hedland is like that.

Dustman's Drama

My Old Man

Several of the town's school teachers decided to form
Port Hedland Drama Club, and as I had acted at school,
I joined up. We would rehearse for six months and then
put on a new play; looking back I can't imagine where I
found time.

My problem was remembering lines but song lyrics
were a bit easier; probably because they used rhyme
and had a rhythm. The club decided to stage a variety
show and being the town's rubbish man, a certain song
seemed like a good idea. I got dressed up as a dustman
and sang *My Old Man's a Dustman*; it went down well
with the Port Hedland crowd.

We are sitting in the audience's seats; Mum, Karen
and me, at the hall in town. Dad is going to come on
soon. It's a variety night at the Drama Club and there
has been a singer, then three people did some acting
about being in a bus stop and waiting for the bus that
didn't come, and there was a funny person who told
us jokes.

On stage the lights are low and the woman who
introduces the acts is talking about a dustman! We
are clapping like crazy because the lights have come
on and Dad is on stage. He looks so funny; he's got

shorts on, a bright yellow plastic raincoat and hat. Dangling from his hat are seven or eight sticky fly strips. These are used in our house to catch the flies, who like the way they smell and get stuck on them. All of his strips are covered in flies! As he moves his head from side-to-side, the strips and the flies flick around making a rustling noise. Oops! One of the strips has stuck to another one and he's trying to unstick them; everyone chuckles at the face he's pulling. Now the music starts and Dad is singing 'My Old Man's a Dustman.' Well, my old man is a dustman; the best dustman of Port Hedland; ever!

He's moving around the stage singing and as he does a little dance over on the side, the fly strips get even more tangled. He just keeps on singing. It's nearly the end of the song and he sings, "Don't kick him in the dustbin, it might be my old dad." and everyone claps and we cheer. That's our Dad! He smiles, waves and then walks off stage; then he pokes his head back around the corner and waggles his fly strips. Ha-ha! I love you Dad.

Molly's Salon

32 Edgar Street

Number thirty two Edgar Street was a simple building with a gable roof and corrugated iron awning out front, supported by four white steel posts. It was clad with asbestos-cement wall sheeting, painted light green and raised about four hundred millimetres up off the ground on thick concrete stumps. Three hardwood steps led up to a centrally placed front door and either side were two small windows. In previous years it had been a Roman Catholic church but now, it was unused.

I had heard that the old church building was up for rent and I though about moving Molly's hairdressing out of the house by fitting out a salon in the building. This was great and I talked with Molly about the project. She liked the idea, so we went and met with the priest and signed up for the road frontage area; the remainder of the building was being divided and rented out to other businesses. Port Hedland Taxis was down the side, and McCullock Outboards and Bridgestone Motor Cycles were taking some space too.

We worked out how much floor space we'd need and, in my spare time, I partitioned it off. Molly organised new equipment to be sent up from Perth—three of the latest hair dryers, makeup stations, basins, chairs, a reception counter and most important, air conditioning! We put new linoleum sheeting down on the floor, painted the inside walls and ceilings, put up mirrors, extra power points, ran new plumbing and fitted the air conditioner into one of the small side window openings. We also got a new phone number for the salon, it was one hundred and eighty one.

The final touch was a large sign, full width across the awning, and in the summer of 1968 it was all ready; we opened *Molly's Salon*, the first ever ladies hairdressing salon in Port Hedland. Molly was in business!

Molly's Salon in Edgar Street.

I'm sitting in Mum's salon, in one of the hairdressing chairs where the ladies get their hair done up. It's nice and cool in here, and bright, and everything is new. Sometimes Mum cuts my hair in here.

There is a big appointment book on the counter and on the front of the counter a picture of the ocean; it goes the whole way across. Mum is cleaning up and then we can go home. I came in after school. She has wiped down all the tops and swept all of the hair from the floor. It looks so neat and clean. And the big funny hair dryers are lined up along a wall; they look like bubble-headed aliens. I tried one out and they are hot. Maybe the women could just put their head out the window for a while and dry their hair. Down at the other end of the room are all the basins where the hair washing is done. It's a lot of stuff just for hair!

Mum is nearly done; she's turning off the lights and the air conditioner. I hope they get air conditioning at my school soon.

During my rubbish round I was able to call in at seven o'clock in the morning and switch on the air conditioner, so that when Molly started work at nine the salon was cool to go into. Business increased as word got around and the ladies found the new salon. A lot of her trade came from the barmaids as well as town folks, and some of the women travelled great distances to have their hair done, and had even stayed overnight at our house.

The travelling hairdressers still called into Port Hedland throughout the year, and Molly found that women would come to her to have their hair repaired, after receiving poor work from the traveller. She had joined the Country Women's Association (CWA) and during a meeting stood up to talk to the association about supporting local businesses, particularly those run by women. My wife was influential and shortly after her talk, the visiting hairdressers were discouraged from coming and eventually bypassed the town.

It wasn't long before she needed some help and Molly recruited one of the barmaids from The Esplanade Hotel who had hairdressing experience and another girl part-time; she was now working with Judy and Joy. We discovered, as staff came and went over the months and years, that it was a constant battle to get good staff who would stay and work in Port Hedland. We had to offer keen rates of pay, as an incentive to get them to come and work for just a three month trial.

Stephen Outram

The Town Passes Us By

Living in the Suburbs

Port Hedland was experiencing massive growth; the population was expanding rapidly and my floor tiling work was growing as more builders came into the town and new houses sprang up. When we had first bought our land it was located one and a half kilometres out of town, now Port Hedland had swallowed up the house and gone way passed us. We were no longer out of town; we were living in the suburbs. Now, we had neighbours to the side and across Brearley Street; fortunately the block on our northerly side remained vacant, which was handy for parking the vehicles and rubbish truck, and Stephen had been growing watermelons along the property line.

My watermelons are getting really big; one is huge. I've been growing them near the soakage trench that drains from our house, so they get water. I've picked the huge one and Mum has to come and help me carry it onto the verandah. We take it to Richardson's Butcher Shop; they buy my watermelons. The butcher weighs it on his big scales. Wow! It weighs over twenty five kilograms; the butcher says that's fifty two pounds in old measurement. He pays me two dollars and fifty cents. Mum asks me what I'm going to spend my money on and I'm not sure; I might keep it for a while.

Two-storey houses had become popular and linoleum was the fashionable floor covering. Laying this type of floor covering involved sanding down the timber floors and cleaning up all of the dust, then large rolls of linoleum were cut with knives and glued down to the floor. I had a heavy floor roller, which helped to smooth out any air pockets trapped under the sheet and create a good contact with the glue. The difficult part of a house were its hallways, which always had three or four doorways along them; the sheeting had to be laid in one long strip and it was a skilled job to cut-in around all of the architraves and openings, and achieve a neat finish. When we were done, I swept and cleaned the floor ready for its new owners. I got Derek to help me with two-storey houses because the heavy linoleum rolls had to be lifted upstairs.

In addition to the growing demand for floor tiling, as the population grew so did the number of rubbish bins to be emptied. Once again I found my life to be consumed by work and mainly saw the family during dinner times. It was tough for all of us as the children were growing fast and Molly was busy with the salon.

During the summer months I was starting at four thirty in the morning; by eleven o'clock the truck's steering wheel was too hot to handle and so I packed it in and went back to work at two in the afternoon. When my run was finished, I went tiling until six in the evening and then went home to put dinner on; Molly was also finishing in the salon at six so we were able to have dinner together. After dinner we would wash all the salon's towels ready for use the next day.

I really needed some needed help and asked Derek,

who was now working on the wharfs as Topman. He was a single guy, but reliable and it worked out well. We arranged that on the first week I drive and he would lift the bins and then we alternated the roles after that. I was lucky to have him and Candy liked him too—we had a great team of three.

Working with Derek, we were able to finish the run by late morning and then I was free to begin my new tiling work just after lunch; and because I was tiling inside, under cover, handling the heat was much easier.

Molly was concerned about our two children; Stephen was now ten and Karen eight years old. She worried that we were working so much and there was no one home when they finished school. I really didn't know what to do and left her with it.

I'm sitting in the bathroom waiting for Mum to come home; my leg is bleeding and I'm holding it with my hands. It hurts a lot. I was playing with my friends at their house, across the vacant block. We had accidently locked ourselves out of the house and their parents were not home. The bathroom window was open but it's higher than I can reach. So, I squatted right down and then jumped up high to grab the sill. As I jumped, the metal ant capping on top of a nearby stump ripped a long hole in my thigh. When I looked into the hole I could see the fatty tissue; it's deep. I ran home straight away but no one was here. I washed the cut with water from the tap and put one of Mum's small hairdressing towels around my leg, like a bandage. There's a low stool in our bathroom and I'm sitting on that.

My leg is throbbing; no one is here yet; I'll just wait.

I can hear Mum coming in and I yell out to her; I start crying a bit. She opens the towel, looks at the hole and says that we have to go to hospital. I tell her what happened as she dials the telephone and calls a taxi; he gets us there quickly. We had to wait a while but now we are in the surgery and the doctor tells me it will need stitches. It stings really bad when he sticks the needle in, to numb the area. Now it doesn't hurt so much and I ask if I can help. He gets me to push the sides of the cut together and starts stitching up my skin. He talks and tells me what he's doing, with the little knots. He says that it has to stay stitched for a few weeks and then I can come back and see him again, to get them out.

My thigh has a thin red line on it with the little stitches; they feel funny. He tells me there's to be no jumping around for a while and to take care of it. He doesn't want to see me back here with any broken stitches! Yes sir.

My leg begins to hurt again. Mum says I've been brave and we go home. At home she's a bit angry and tells me that if anything like that happens again I must ring her at work and she will come. I hadn't even thought about the telephone and just went into the bathroom; that's where we normally handle the cuts and bruises.

When I got home Stephen proudly showed me his stitches and he explained what had happened. He stayed home from school, limped around for several days and the wound pulled together and began to heal;

he was careful and the stitches held.

After that Molly scheduled extra staff hours at the salon so she could leave earlier. She was concerned that there was no one home when the children finished school, and from then on we arranged that one of us would be; though that mostly fell to her.

What Camel?

The One That Almost Wasn't

Early one morning, in the dark, I drove the rubbish truck down a laneway and had to slam on the brakes; there in the headlights was a camel! Candy the dog barked and I blew the horn, but the camel stood its ground. In the end I had to enter the laneway at each of its ends, to work around the stubborn camel and clear the rubbish bins.

When I got home for breakfast I told Molly about the camel; she scoffed and remarked that it was just another one of my fancy stories. So, I asked her to ask her customers; perhaps someone had seen the camel and could corroborate my story. When she got home that night I asked her if anyone knew about the camel. She told me that no one knew about a camel, no one had seen a camel and there was no camel except in my imagination. I began to wonder if there was a camel at all; if only our clever dog could speak English.

A couple of months later I was contracted to do a floor tiling job at the Pardoo Roadhouse & Tavern, which was a pub one hundred and fifty kilometres along the road to Broome. I got there about four o'clock in the afternoon, had a look at the job and prepared it all ready for the next day.

Dinner at home was at six o'clock and I had some time
to kill, so I had a look around. When I got around
to the back of the building there was a big surprise. I
found my missing camel!

I was so excited that I ran to get my camera out of the
car and ran back to take some photographs for proof;
the camel seemed to take it all in his stride. I went and
sought out the owner; he confirmed that his camel had
been in Port Hedland. They had been out to the horse
races at Broome and had a stopover in Port Hedland.
They'd tied the camel up overnight in the lane to keep
him out of the way. The next morning they were up
early, loaded the camel into their ute and left before
six in the morning; and that's why no one had seen it,
except Candy and I.

All of our photographs had to be sent to Perth for
developing, so I had to wait patiently for over a month
to finish the film, get it developed and have the slides
sent back to Port Hedland. Then, one evening after
dinner I quietly set up the projector and slipped in the
best camel shot.

Karen and I are helping Mum clean up after dinner,
taking the plates to the kitchen. She starts washing
up. Dad is in the lounge room setting up the slide
projector and screen; a new box of slides has come
and we are excited to see them. He has turned his
back to us and is looking through the slides, holding
them up to the light. Normally he waits until we
are all ready; normally he's telling us to hurry up so
we can begin the show, but tonight Dad is a bit too
quiet. What's he up to?

160

When everyone was seated and ready for the show, with great drama I switched on the projector. Ta-da! There was my camel. When I showed Molly and the kids the photographs and told them all the *Camel That Nearly Wasn't* story, we all had a good laugh!

Slide nights were something that we all enjoyed and I was good at telling a story or two to go along with the pictures. From the time I loaded a new film in the camera, then took thirty six shots, had them developed in Perth and got them back, several months might have gone by. Often, we had little idea about what was on the film, especially if Molly had taken some shots too. It was also interesting to see if the shots actually worked: underexposed, overexposed or actually getting the subject in-frame.

There was great excitement in the Outram's house when one of those little rectangular boxes arrived in our mail. Even in later years, those gatherings in the dark around the slide projector were memorable and fun family events. Sometimes I struggled to get the little paper slide cases in the slot, put them in upside-down or back-to-front, or dropped them on the floor and then couldn't find them in the dark; and the "Oohs" and "Aahs" when something special popped up on-screen— it was all part of the show. And I was very grateful for the camera that we brought with us from Aden, which had faithfully captured much of our early story in Australia, particularly the first five years.

Growing Pains

New House Guests

Molly's Salon was becoming well known in the town and surrounding areas, and the appointment book was full all week. She needed extra staff, but when the occasional hairdresser blew into town from Perth they asked for big city wages. Their rates gave us a shock but Molly had little choice; her work load was increasing.

As hairdressers came and went she ran advertisements in the Perth newspapers and picked up who she could, which wasn't always ideal. We put up our prices in the salon and received some complaints from the locals; unfortunately for them our running costs had to be met or Molly would not be staying in business for long. After a while we realised that staffing was always going to be somewhat irregular and this was simply part of living in a remote area; Port Hedland was not everyone's cup-of-tea. We discussed what kind of incentives could be offered to make working here easier and more attractive.

Accommodation in the town was in short supply and so we offered hairdressers a room in our house as part of a three month contract working at the salon, which proved to work well in getting the women to town. We could bundle the children together and free-up our third bedroom when it was required for a guest.

During the summer, Karen and I often sleep on
the verandah, where it's cooler; we put our fold-up
beds out there and sleep under sheets. Mum and
Dad sometimes use my room for the hairdressers or
one of Mum's clients from out of town and I put
my clothes in Karen's room. I don't mind sharing
my room and sometimes the visitors play cards,
and Scrabble or Monopoly with us. We like playing
games. We listen to their stories about living on a
station with cattle and horses, or about Perth. I asked
the Perth girls if my surfboard was safe at the Manly
Hostel, but they didn't know.

Stephen and Karen got on well together so sharing a
room wasn't a problem and often, they enjoyed someone
new in the house. In fact, we all did as it provided
a connection with the city; discussions about new
fashions, hair styles, new shops, films and life in the
capital were refreshing. It reminded us that we'd only
explored a small part of Australia and it was a very
big place; and I suspect it planted the seeds of a much
needed holiday and the possibility of something in our
future, beyond Port Hedland.

Stephen Outram

Shopping Smart

Fresh Produce

We began to look for a better way of getting our fruit
and vegetables, as prices in Port Hedland were very
high. A group of us got together and obtained the
services of a green grocer, who was located in Perth.
We would all put in for a standard fixed-dollar-amount
order and the grocer would make us up a package of
seasonal produce, which was trucked up every week. The
order would arrive at our house and members of the
group came by to pick up their share. As we didn't know
exactly what was in the boxes, it was always some fun
unpacking them and discovering what we'd been sent.
The grocer billed us monthly and the system worked
very well. Occasionally, during the cyclone season, the
truck couldn't get through and we'd lose that order.
Even with the losses, it worked out much cheaper than
buying locally in Port Hedland.

After a while we expanded the idea further to include
general household items. We located a big Perth store
and put in orders for cartons of Fanta or Coca Cola,
Heinz Baked Beans, tins of powdered milk, cleaning
gear and the like; they would ship it all up to us and
then we distributed it throughout the group.

We ran out of Fanta. Fanta is my favourite drink and
I have to wait until our new order comes in, and then

164

I have to wait until it goes in the refrigerator and gets cold, and I'll probably be at school then so I'll have to wait until I get home and then I can have a Fanta.

It was a lot of work handling the orders when they were delivered, but it provided a significant financial saving for everyone. Considering the local shops were probably doing something similar, we were able to sidestep their markup.

And in a similar way to having hairdressing staff from Perth stay at our house, it strengthened our connection with life beyond Port Hedland—that we were able to reach beyond the limited facilities, intense heat, numerous flies and beyond the isolation, was a great comfort.

Mum got an ice cream maker from Perth. She puts in powered milk and sugar and turns it on. When the ice cream is ready she pours it into her Tupperware (she loves Tupperware) popsicle makers and puts a handle on the end; they all stand upsidedown in a ho.der tray and then go in the freezer. She makes cordial flavoured ice popsicles too, and Karen and I eat as many as we can!

Stephen Outram

Walking for the Doctor

One Dollar per Kilometre

It's morning assembly and the school's principal is
announcing that there is going to be a twenty five
kilometre walk, to raise money for the Royal Flying
Doctor Service. He is saying that all of the kids are
invited to join in and begin getting pledges of money
for each kilometre we walk. I'm doing it!

Stephen came home from school and told us that he
was going on a charity walk for the Flying Doctor
and asked us to pledge some money. It seemed like a
good idea and I figured he'd soon get bored walking
around the town in circles, so I signed for one dollar per
kilometre; Molly was smarter than me and offered to
take his sheet into work.

Mum has taken my pledge sheet into the salon and
asked her clients for their support; she got heaps of
names. I went around to my friend's parents houses
and got some pledges, though some said they are
supporting their own kids. I asked Dad's mate Derek
and Mr. Nichols, and they both pledged.

I was working throughout the day and then meeting
up with some of the wharfies I knew afterwards, as one
of them was leaving Port Hedland and heading back
to Perth; his farewell was at the Esplanade Hotel. I

166

arranged to meet the family in town, to go out for the evening meal and we would see how Stephen had done.

Today is Saturday and everyone is assembled near the Pier Hotel; it's 8:00 a.m. There are a lot of people here: children, adults, dogs, people in wheelbarrows, some wearing costumes, several runners and a lot of my friends from school too. There's a red tape strung up across the road and the starter has his cap gun raised up in the air. Ready, steady, go! We're off!

Everyone is excited and we are pushing and tripping each other and generally, mucking around. There's lots of chatter, laughing and some people start singing. My friends and I follow the crowd around. We're all walking along The Esplanade and turn onto Richardson Street to go along the beach; then we are on Kingsmill and go all the way along Sutherland Street before turning back towards town.

The course goes right past my house and I walk around a couple of times and then stop in at home. No one is here; Karen has gone into the salon with Mum and Dad is working. I have a drink and some lunch. Out through the sliding glass doors I can see people still walking past and I'm bored at home so I go and walk some more. My friends seemed to have gone but I keep on going. In the end I do eighteen kilometres and finish the day with sore legs and sunburn.

Mum comes home with Karen and we clean up and go to meet Dad in town for dinner; I'm hungry. Dad asks how far I walked and I tell him eighteen. He's surprised. He says he's proud of me and, as a treat, he's going to get me a t-bone steak for dinner. He goes off to order the meals.

We're having our dinner and Dad is sitting next to me; he's talking a lot. It's funny because he is repeating himself and talking really slow. Mum's across the table, she looks at me and rolls her eyes; I'm not sure what that means. She leans over, close, and whispers that my father has been drinking. I'm still confused. Drinking? Tea? Fanta? And then one of Dad's wharfie mates comes over with a bottle of Emu Bitter in his hand and I catch on. Ahhh … that kind of drinking. My Dad is pissed!

Landlord

Easy Money

Next to Molly's Salon, in Edgar Street, was a spare block of land that also belonged to the church; I approached the priest to see if it was for rent; it was and I managed to get a six month lease, ongoing if required, and placed an advertisement in several of Perth's major newspapers.

> Vacant land for rent, Central Port Hedland, W.A. 12M road frontage. Telephone: 181.

A caravan company, Aristocrat Caravans from Brisbane, Queensland contacted me; they were interested in having a presence in the area and wanted a yard to display their range of products. They could run their local office right out of one of the vans, on-site, and just needed power and water. It was easy enough to run a power cable across from the salon, a water pipe from the outside tap, and they would make their own arrangements for a telephone service. We agreed on a price per month, for a six month lease, ongoing if needed; and so we made some easy money for doing very little!

Aristocrat ended up staying with us the whole time we had Molly's Salon. It was a good arrangement and my first venture as landlord.

Stephen Outram

Shark Rescue

Too Close for Comfort

Last night Dad and I went fishing off the jetty. It was
unusual but there were no ships in, so we had lots
of room at the main wharf and there were no safety
rails to fish over; it was open to the harbour. The tide
was running out fast and perfect for whiskers salmon;
the water, some six metres below us, was just a dull
glimmer in the jetty's lights.

Dad had a forty five kilogram breaking strain line
wound around a large red hand reel, a big sinker to
handle the swift current and a decent sized hook
threaded with fresh mullet that I'd caught earlier in
the day. He unwound some of the line and let it drop
down loosely on the deck and then began swinging
the rig around his head, gradually letting line out and
increasing its radius. When he had a fair speed up and
the line was whistling through the air he let it all go
and the hook, bait and sinker arched out over the
water, disappearing into the dark; we heard it splash.
He let the line run out with the tide and then looped
it around one of the jetty's thick timber piles and put
the reel down on the deck. He came over and gave
me a hand to cast my own line, then went further
along to throw out a third line and we were all set.

It wasn't long before one of his farthest lines took

off and Dad hauled in a medium sized salmon; he
re-baited the hook once again and swung it out
deep into the harbour. About twenty minutes later
the big line took off and bracing his foot against the
wharf's solid edge-beam, he carefully unwound it
from around the pile and began hauling in his fish. It
fought hard and he was sweating by the time it neared
the jetty and broke surface, kicking water everywhere.
I had a torch shining down the six metre drop and we
saw that he'd hooked a metre long baby shark, which
was threshing against the piles.

Dad cursed; a shark was not what he wanted. He
hauled on the thick line and lifted the shark up above
the surface. Before he was able to take another hand
hold, a huge grey adult shark surged up out of the
water, severed the line with one bite and a shake of
its head, and freed the baby. They both hit the water
with a great splash and were gone in an instant. I
nearly dropped the torch as suddenly, six metres
seemed not much distance at all! Dad had been taking
the strain and leaning out over the edge to see down
as he lifted; the powerful tug from the shark's bite
had unbalanced him and for a moment he swayed
further out. When the line snapped, he suddenly
fell backwards onto the wharf; the hand reel hit the
deck, rattled off and rolled away for a distance before
settling.

We looked at each other in silence for a moment and
then, without a word, began to wind in the lines and
packed up our gear. When we were done, we threw
the spare bait out into the water and then walked
along the jetty and out to the where our car was

parked, near the Esplanade Hotel. When we got into the car Dad looked at me and laughed in relief, and then we drove home.

We didn't tell Mum the story for a few days and, as expected, she was horrified. For a while, I had to sneak out to go fishing at the jetty and not tell her. Ever since the Finucane Island skiing trip with Tony Wiles, she's had a morbid fear of things in the ocean that have teeth, which is most things.

Making a Splash

Hedland's First Pool

With the coming of summer 1967, we saw an above-ground swimming pool kit advertised in a catalogue. No one had a swimming pool in Port Hedland. The catalogue described a six by two and a half metre pool, with a deck on one side, water pump and filter; we liked the idea and sent off for it.

When the kit arrived, I borrowed a tractor with a digging bucket on it and a tip truck from Ken Nichols and dug the backyard down about half a metre; Derek and I fitted the pool kit together one afternoon. We laid down a fine-sand base to protect and level the lining. The pool had a deck one side to sit on, which we fitted last and when it was all ready the hose went in; it took ages and ages to fill. We used it for the first time on Boxing Day.

Dad's been digging up the backyard for our new swimming pool. I can't wait! Derek and Dad took the side fence down and have been using a red tractor with a bucket, to scoop dirt out and dump it in one of Mr. Nichols' big trucks. Wow; there's a lot of dirt in a backyard!

Now the hole is ready and the pool wall is going up; it's a silver, metal sheet about one metre high that is clipped into posts. They are putting sand down on the bottom and smoothing it out ready for the pool lining. The plastic lining is all one piece, it goes across the floor, up the silver wall and over the top. Dad gets me to put the hose pipe in and turn on the tap, and water is trickling across the beautiful blue lining. Dad is in there, bare feet, pulling the lining out so it lies flat. Now, a metal capping presses down on top of the walls, all the way around, and is bolted to the posts. The water is running really slow; it's going to take a long time before we can have a swim.

As the water comes up on the inside, Dad and I are shovelling dirt back-in, around the outside. The water and dirt balance each other out so the pool sides stay upright. It's taken four days to fill the pool but now the backyard is level again and the grass can go in. The pool looks like it's in the ground.

Dad's put a sitting board up on one side, nearest the house, and Candy is up there. She's asking if she can go for a swim. Dad tells her no; Candy's claws might tear the plastic lining and she has to stay out. He's going to put the fence back up soon or all the dogs will be coming in for a swim.

It looks so beautiful and blue, and there's a red and yellow blowup ball skimming across the water. This is the first swimming pool in Port Hedland. All the other kids love me!

Boy! Did we become popular with kids once the word got out; they were queuing up at the door and I started charging admission (only kidding!). Birthdays and parties were especially exciting; we held races,

174

tied balloons all the way around and I used to throw in handfuls of coins to be retrieved from the bottom. Stephen was like a fish and always took a good share. Our swimming pool proved to be a great success!

Karen and I are having a swim after dinner; it's dark now and we can see all the way up to the stars. We are floating on our lie-lows and look out over the fence. Big surprise; we can see the drive-in screen from our pool! The drive-in is just down the road and the big screen stands up really tall. We can watch films, but there's no sound. I talk with Karen about how we could get some long pieces of wire, sneak over to the drive-in and borrow a speaker; then bring it back to our place and hook it over the fence so we can hear too. I'll check it out tomorrow; Mum's calling and it's time for bed now.

The swimming pool was a great attraction and a popular feature of our house until later in the year. The Shire Council had built a public pool out on Crawford Street and named it in honour of Percy Gratwick; a Victoria Cross recipient from World War II. It had a twenty five metre main pool and a separate deep water pool, with one metre and three metre high diving boards.

Stephen and Karen went to the public pool because all of their friends were there; and the schools used it for water sports. Both children swam strongly in many swimming events, and got their life saving medals at Gratwick. I was particularly pleased when Stephen took out the school's high diving competition with an impressive one and a half forward roll off the ten metre board—I had dived competitively too, for the Royal Navy in England. When he was presented with his

175

trophy, I remembered that little boy, on Fairsky, coming to tell us that he could swim; and now he was winning competitions!

I'm practicing my diving in the deep pool. I've just come up from a dive and swum over to the side. A woman is there and she is covering her mouth with her hand. She is saying something to me but I can't hear because her hand is in the way. She pulls her hand aside and her mouth looks strange. I look at her mouth and I can see she has no teeth. She's telling me she has lost her teeth in the pool. What? Really?

I do a duck dive and swim down and I can see the teeth sitting on the bottom. How does someone lose their teeth? I run out of breath, it's three metres deep, and go up to the surface again. I get my breath back and tell her that I saw the teeth. She is very exited and asks me if I will go back and get them. I take a big breath and swim down again. The teeth look very creepy sitting on the bottom of the pool. I close my eyes, reach out and pick them up, and then push off from the bottom holding on tightly to the teeth; I don't want to drop them and have to do this again. I give the lady her teeth and she smiles (I wish she hadn't) and thanks me. She swims off with her teeth in-hand and climbs out of the diving pool. How did her teeth come out? I'll have to ask Mum; she'll know.

Holidays 1968

Back to Cottesloe

In late 1968 I managed to organise a break from work and took the family on our second holiday to Cottesloe Beach. Unfortunately for the kids it was during the school term and we had made arrangements for them to attend a local primary school. This time we flew down with MacRobertson Miller Airlines and had a weekend together at the Manley Hostel before they started class.

We have a different room this time at the Manly, but Karen and I are still sleeping on the verandah. I'm going down the back steps to the storage room and the door is unlocked. I go inside to get my surfboard, but it's not there. Aww!

On Monday morning we caught a bus and took Karen and Stephen to the Cottesloe Primary School, in Keane Street. It was a beautiful old brick building with high pitched roofs and magnificent arched openings along the front. Neither of the kids were very happy about going to school during their holiday but we got them registered and settled in. After a few days of school I began to realise how far behind, in their education, the children had fallen during the last three years at Port Hedland. Both Molly and I spent some time with them, in the evenings, assisting with their homework.

I have no idea what the teacher is talking about; we haven't done this work at my school. The other kids think I'm a dumb boy down from the bush.

I've been asked to stand up at the front and give a talk about Port Hedland: I'm telling them about the Aboes and because they like to go walkabout, and leave their jobs, businesses pay them low wages. This year, a law was passed where Aboes had to be paid at the same rate as white people, but the Aboes work differently and businesses don't like to pay them the full rate. A boy calls out and says that Australian Aborigines are as good as whites and should get paid the same! I'm telling him that he should go and live in Port Hedland and see for himself! The teacher says for everyone to be quiet and I can go and sit down.

Some of the lessons, like maths, are really hard and I'm doing extra work to catch up with the other kids. Today, we are doing a class about space and the solar system and the teacher has put up a big picture showing all the planets going around the sun. Now we have to write an essay about it; all I can think of is Will Robinson and the Robot yelling, "Danger! Danger!" but I know she won't like that very much.

After a while the kids seemed to have settled into school and made some new friends, and we enjoyed Cottesloe with them when they returned each afternoon. I bought Stephen a new foam surfboard and he was so excited that he even gave up *Lost in Space* to go surfing! During the day Molly and I enjoyed the beach, read and relaxed. On the weekend we took the kids to Kings Park and saw the floral clock, where we waited to hear the native bird calls on the half hour.

We also explored a huge thirty two metre long Karri log, had some lunch in a nearby cafe and then walked around the Botanic Gardens.

Another day we went to Beatty Park swimming pools and Stephen climbed right up to the top of the Olympic diving platform to have a look, but came down to the three metre level before he dived.

After we were all so suntanned that our teeth looked brilliant white and the kids hair had gone blonde, and we had done lots of sightseeing around Perth, our holidays came to an end. Stephen wasn't leaving his surfboard behind this time, and we managed to get it aboard the flight and up to Port Hedland, where it lived in the swimming pool.

All too soon I was back at work, but I sent our holiday photographs off to Perth for developing and we devoured those delicious Cottesloe Beach shots at the next family slide show.

Race Day

A Dollar Each Way

A city person would probably be amused by the relief, distraction and excitement that a large annual event like Race Day brings to a remote community. One could be forgiven for thinking that it's a horse race, rather than a social event that brings people together from far and wide, to have some fun. In locations where neighbours are distant, trips to town rare and single people somewhat isolated it should be no surprise to find that new relationships, marriages and sometimes unplanned babies have resulted from attending a Race Day.

The horse racing season began in early winter at Onslow and worked upward through Roebourne, Port Hedland, Marble Bar, Derby, Fitzroy Crossing, Wyndham, Hall's Creek and across the Northern Territory border. The horses were often from local stations and jockeys were station boys or stock men, wearing a satin jacket and flying colors, who competed for a brief chance of glory in the long year. Some professional jockeys and their horses traveled from town-to-town, as did the bookmakers, intent on their business of odds, bets and making money.

Race Day was a big deal in the North West and with the Port Hedland Race Club being one of the town's first institutions, founded in 1896; the day was a major annual event for the town.

Molly and I were not really into horses or racing but we went; it was very nice to drive there in our new car. I'd recently bought us a Holden HD station wagon; it was light blue, had lots of room for the family and I could lay down the back seat and get all of my work gear in there. The yellow ute was getting quite worn out and becoming unreliable; I was lucky to sell it on for fifty dollars.

Tony and Jean were waiting for us in the carpark and we went in together; we met just about every other person we knew, there as well, and the children seemed to make new friends as there was a mob of them running around together. It was a very social and enjoyable day and I even bet a dollar each way in the Hedland Cup. I put some fifty cent bets on for Karen and Stephen and they ran out to the rails to cheer for their horses when they raced. Unfortunately, I didn't pick any winners.

At Port Hedland's Race Day, in addition to horse racing, the locals participated in foot races, tug-of-war competitions, a few fights, barbecues and a ball. All of the ladies had sent off to Perth for fancy hats, race frocks, frills, nylon stockings and fine shoes; that were soon covered with a layer or three of red dust, but none seemed to mind. The day culminated in a splendid gala evening with plenty of beer, music and dancing.

We're doing a tug-of-war, where the townies kids are taking on the out-of-town kids. There's more of us than them, so, me and some of the townies get into the out-of-town's team to even up the numbers.

181

The rope is thick with knots in it, one for each person, and a ribbon tied in the middle. The kids are mucking around and pretending to fall over; we're not even started yet. Now we're ready and the starter man tells us to take the strain. The rope comes up off the ground, straightens up and he yells out for us to start.

We all pull hard and lean back, my feet are slipping in rubber thongs and I kick them off and dig in with my heels and toes. The red dust is coming up and we get pulled forward a bit and then a boy in the back bellows out for us to pull, and we all do.

He's got a big voice and yells out again and again and again; we get a good rhythm going. We're working together now and gain some ground. One of our boys slips on loose gravel and falls, but he gets up quickly and we keep on going. Suddenly, the other team lets go and we all tumble backwards and fall to the ground; arms and legs everywhere. The dust comes up over us, but we've won! Our team, the townies and the out-of-towns, has beaten the townies. Hooray!

I learned to play the Australian game of Two Up on the floor of a bar. Bets were laid and then two copper pennies were spun, up into the air, and allowed to fall to the floor; it didn't seem to matter whether they landed heads or tails, I lost my money. I was amused to see the local police were running the game.

Race Day was a real party day with plenty of Swan Lager and Emu Bitter downed and everybody joined in; even the priest was down at the track cooking steaks on a barbecue! We didn't stay late at the race track or attend the ball that night as I had to get up early for work, and we wanted to get the children home. When I did my rubbish run the next morning, it was very quiet in Port Hedland and I suspected there were quite a few sore heads being nursed.

Stephen Outram

News From Space

Australia First

Everyone is quiet in our classroom. Over the
blackboard, high up on the wall there is a loudspeaker
and the principal has just finished talking to us. Now
we can hear a different voice; it's an American voice.

This morning at assembly the principal announced
that there would be a special broadcast at 10:50 a.m.
and we would need to be in the classrooms to hear it.
He told us that three hundred and eighty thousand
kilometres above Earth, the Apollo 11 mission would
be landing on the moon, something that has never
been done before; the school was going to listen to
history in the making. He said that it was important
for Australia because CSIRO's Parkes radio telescope
is going to be the first to receive the transmission and
then send it all around the world.

I can hear some voices; they sound is scratchy but
it's the astronauts talking to mission control. They
are landing and giving lots of measurements about
the distance Apollo is from the moon's surface. In
the background I can hear their rockets. We've been
listening for about five minutes now, and one of
them says there's three feet to go; another voice calls
out thirty seconds. Then the first voice says that the
engines have stopped and our teacher starts clapping

and says that they are down. Wow! We all cheer.

The principal comes back on and says we can go back to work now, but our teacher talks about Apollo 11 and the mission for a while. One boy asks why they went to the moon and teacher says that the Americans wanted to beat the Russians in the race to space; I guess it's a bit like sport's day.

The 26th Parallel

Time to Go

The 26th Parallel crosses the North West Coastal Highway, in Western Australia, twenty six degrees south of the equator. Further east, it defines the border between the Northern Territory and South Australia, and a small portion of Queensland's border. To many Western Australians, the area above this imaginary line is known as The North West and in the minds of some it is, unofficially, another state of Australia.

Not long after Christmas 1968 Molly said she thought that it was time we got away from Port Hedland, before it killed us. I gave it serious thought and she was quite right. She was now employing two full-time hairdressers and working the salon six days a week; and I would soon need two rubbish trucks and men to go with them. We were both extremely tired; Molly looked haggard and I was skin and bones.

We heard on Port Hedland's grapevine that the hospital was looking for a doctor's residence, and we put forward Number Two Brearley Street to be considered by the Ministry of Health. A Ministry officer was touring towns in Western Australia's northwest, assessing property, but it was several months before he was due in Port Hedland. When he did arrive, the house was inspected and he liked what he saw. We agreed to leave it fully furnished and settled on a price of twenty seven thousand dollars. After paying off our debts we were left with twenty two thousand dollars; a small fortune at the time.

I did not renew my contracts with the Shire Council and they were most unhappy that I was leaving; they had enjoyed reliable and trouble free service for the past three years. My friend Derek wouldn't take it on and went back to work at the wharf.

Molly's Salon proved difficult to sell; neither of the staff were interested in running their own business and we ended up almost giving it away for the price of the stock and equipment.

And so it came to pass that early one winter's morning in August 1969, we put our suitcases, the children and Candy the dog into our Holden station wagon. I closed the driveway gate and said goodbye to the house I'd built; we made our way out onto Wilson Street, drove over the causeway and then turned right for Perth.

We drove south from Port Hedland eight hundred kilometres along the North West Coastal Highway, to Canarvon where we stopped for the night. The next morning we were off early and after a several hours found the 26th Parallel, marked by a simple black and white road sign. The sign read:

"26TH PARALLEL
LEAVING THE NORTH - WEST"

I pulled the car over to take a photograph. We all held hands and ceremonially stepped over the 26th Parallel and then got back in to the car and drove away. I found my sense of adventure returning and planted the accelerator to the floor; with a hearty cheer we roared off towards Perth and whatever was beyond that.

Forty five years later I still have that photograph, and I will keep it with me until the day I die. It reminds me of a time that I will never have to live again, and one that I'm very proud to have chosen.

Epilogue

Final Thoughts

We drove all the way to Canarvon and stayed the night at a roadside motel we knew from previous trips. A tyre had blown and was a difficult roadside repair due to the car being heavily loaded; apart from that the trip was trouble-free. The next day we started out early and that night booked into our old friend, the Manley Hostel at Cottesloe Beach; I noticed that the building was looking worse for wear and was saddened to learn that it would be demolished the next year.

It was mid-winter and the weather was not the best for beach activities; it was overcast and rainy, unlike our previous two holidays. Fortunately though, Doctor Smith, Will Robinson and the Robot were still on television at five o'clock each afternoon for me, and Karen enjoyed reacquainting herself with the daytime shows.

Mum and Dad listed the Perth block of land with a real estate agent and it sold quickly for one thousand four hundred and fifty dollars—Dad's astute contingency, Plan B, was no longer required. Our city friends, Susanna, Peter and their two children had gone to the United States of America; we learned later that they had found there, what they were looking for.

After a week or so in the capital Dad booked us all, including Candy and the car, aboard the great Indian Pacific train to travel east across Australia from the gold town of Kalgoorlie, across the Nullabor Plain and on to Port Augusta in South Australia. From there we drove up into Queensland, as far north as the town of Mackay, and then turned back south to finally settled on the Gold Coast.

One sunny day my parents took Karen and I to the Currumbin Bird Sanctuary, an animal sanctuary, which featured an afternoon feeding of Rainbow Lorikeets. The birds were noisy, voracious feeders and their brilliant plumage was coloured with greens, yellows and oranges. I had seen them just once before; it was on Boxing Day 1964, the day I first climbed SS Fairsky's gangplank and noticed a parrot perched on the ship's rail, peering down at me. I had looked for my Dad, to tell him about the bird but he had gone ...

At the end of his 1965-1970 memoirs my Dad wrote:

"I would like to thank Molly for standing by me during a difficult time; her courage, strength and encouragement was always there to back up the decisions that had to be made.

To my two children, Stephen and Karen, I apologise for not being able to spend quality time with you during the most important part of your lives.

I do not apologise for what I've had to do.

Money did become my main object, to establish
our family in a great and safe country. We were
mainly on our own, with no grandparents to
run-to when times got tough, no baby sitters
to call upon when needed, no dole or any
Government assistance; so if a man didn't work,
his family didn't eat.

I certainly wasn't going back to England saying
that I couldn't make it. We did make it and I
thank you all for standing by me during this
most difficult time."—Trevor Outram, Gold
Coast, 2007

In the writing of this story, I have become aware
that I enjoyed Port Hedland and loved my five years
there. At one point during the research, having been
unable to find much at all about the Junior High
School that Karen and I attended, I discovered four
photographs in the National Archive. And I said,
'Ahh; there you are.' to a dear friend who had gone
missing. Even though the school building has long
been demolished, it was a wonderful moment to
connect with a very joyful part of my life that had
been covered-up under descriptions of hardship and
difficulty. Each member of my family has their own
viewpoint about Port Hedland, but I have no doubt
that it was an extraordinary contribution to all of our
lives and I am very grateful for my first five years in
Australia, and the many that have followed.

But that, as they say, is another story …

Stephen Outram

Fairsky and her Ten Pound Poms

A Little History

SS *Fairsky*

The ship almost began life as 'Steel Artisan.' While being built as a C3 class cargo ship in 1941, the incomplete ship was taken over by the US Government to be used as an escort aircraft carrier. She was loaned to the British Royal Navy, named the HMS Attacker and went on to serve in the North Atlantic, French waters and the Pacific until 1946.

Sitmar Lines acquired the ship in 1952 and in 1957 commissioned the mammoth task of rebuilding her as a passenger liner. Located in New York, USA, she was fitted with a new superstructure and stylish funnel. Maritime Historian, Reuben Goossens notes, "In 1958, she was registered in Liberia with her new name Fairsky."

According to Goossens,[1] Sitmar had obtained the lucrative contract to take British migrants to Australia. Fairsky worked the route between Southampton and

---

1   A Special thanks to Reuben Goossens and his account of Fairsky. You can find out more at ssmaritime.com in his article titled "The Sitmar Ships."

Australia up until 1974.

"The ships of Sitmar Line became a popular
sight in Australian and New Zealand waters."

Thousands of migrants will have enjoyed a drink
and dance in the Lido Lounge and Bar, swum in the
sculptured pool and slept in one of her two, three or
four berth cabins. Fairsky was designed as a cruise ship
and for many, this was the first cruise they had ever
experienced.

Around 1977 Fairsky sailed to Hong Kong for
demolition, but was bought and taken to Manila
to be converted into a floating hotel and casino.
Unfortunately, while nearing completion the ship
caught fire and was totally gutted; the conversion was
abandoned.

She was renamed Fair Sky and towed back to Hong
Kong, to end her days at the breaker's yard in 1979.

Ten Pound Poms

Following the end of World War II, more than a
million people, known as Ten Pound Poms, emigrated
from Britain to Australia. About one quarter of these
returned to the United Kingdom after a couple of years,
but the majority stayed and made Australia home for
themselves, their families and future generations.

Australia's Minister for Immigration, Arthur Calwell,
implemented a scheme designed to substantially
increase the population of Australia. As part of
government's 'Populated or Perish' policy, the assisted
passage scheme ran from 1945 to 1970. Migrants paid

ten pounds per adult, which covered their passage, and agreed to stay in Australia for a minimum of two years.

Advertising in the UK promised good employment prospects, ready housing and an improved lifestyle, though on arrival migrants often discovered otherwise. They were placed in basic hostels, some of which were converted army camps, and left to find their own work. Some people spent their two years in one of these hostels before they went back.

The scheme was not limited to persons from the United Kingdom and was advertised throughout Ireland, Cypress, Malta, Netherlands, Italy, Greece, West Germany and Turkey; it is these migrants that formed the basis for the diverse, multicultural population that Australia enjoys today.

In early 1984 my Dad was asked by a friend why, after adopting Australia as his home for all these years, he had not yet become a citizen. He was somewhat defensive and replied that Australia has his children, was that not enough? Later, my Dad realised that sometimes old loyalties die hard and in March 1984, Molly, Karen and I joined him in applying for Australian Citizenship, and later took the Oath of Allegiance:

> "I, Trevor Reginald Outram, renouncing all other allegiance, swear by Almighty God that I will be faithful and bear true allegiance to Her Majesty Elizabeth the Second, Queen of Australia, Her heirs and successors according to law, and that I will faithfully observe the laws of Australia and fulfil my duties as an Australian

citizen."

We all received our 'Certificate of Australian Citizenship' from Denis O'Connell, Mayor of Gold Coast, on April 30, 1984. Following the ceremony at Surfers Paradise Council Chambers, we went out to lunch together and celebrated two decades, since beginning our first five years at Port Hedland, in 1965.

Stephen Outram

Mrs. Whitty

Poem for a Friend

Circa 1968, Mrs. Whitty[1], who had reached the end of her long life was buried in the Old Pioneer Cemetery near our Brearley Street house. I'm pretty sure that it was a Saturday afternoon that I looked out of our kitchen window and could see the mourners gathered together. I hadn't been told that she had died or was being buried, but I knew it was her.

Mum had asked me to not look and closed the curtain; she was worried I'd be sad, but I stayed at the window for a while longer. Eventually the people went away and the cemetery was quiet. I didn't tell anyone but I went and visited her grave the next day. There was fresh dirt mounded up, a headstone with her name on it and some flowers. I would miss going to her house, chatting and eating the biscuits and cakes she had made; but it was okay.

During my visits to her house, Mrs. Whitty had often spoken of her dead husband, showed me some of his things; photographs, even given me his old golf clubs, and I knew she had gone off to find him. So I looked at her grave in the cemetery, and then went off to the

---

1   I'm not sure of the correct spelling; it may be Whitty or Whittie.

beach for a walk.

In the late nineties, I put together a book of my poetry and included the following one, for my lovely childhood friend.

Mrs. Whittey

I'm not sure why she died
Mrs. Whittey
Maybe she just got old

I only saw the people gathered at her grave
Through the window I saw them
My mother said, "Don't look son"
And pulled the curtain closed

I thought about the friend I'd lost
I should have been there as they lowered her body
into the ground
To say my good-byes, as the others did

I had a right to say goodbye
For she had been kind to an eight year old
Mrs. Whittey

I loved her in my youthful way
And now, at forty years I still remember her
kindness
To a young migrant boy, short of grandmothers

So, for what I didn't say then, I say it now
Goodbye Mrs. Whittey
God bless Mrs. Whittey
Thank you for being my friend.

Stephen Outram

We've Come So Far

A Song of Celebration

Written in August 1994, while living in the United Kingdom, I recorded *We've Come So Far* in 1999 with Mark Bergman at Back Street Studios on the Gold Coast, Australia. The song celebrates my family's immigration and settlement in Australia ... an adventure that began in 1965 and continues on today, and every tomorrow.

Bringing me to Australia was one of the great gifts that my parents gave me. It took a lot of courage to make that move, leave the family 12,000 miles behind in England and then to do whatever it took to get us established. They were true pioneers; I'm grateful for it all.

We've Come So Far[1]

My mother cried, in sixty five
when we left those British Isle
We all held hands, there were no brass bands
as we faced twelve thousand miles

And my Dad stood tall and told us all
of the seeds that we would sow

When we set sail for Australia
all those years ago

And we've come so far, these past fifty years
We've come so far, with all our hopes and all our
fears
We've come so far, to be here today
To see the dream come true
And everyday's Australia Day

A month at sea feeling strange but free
then Rotnest slid slowly by
We docked, down in Fremantle
'neath a cloudless summer sky

And the plane up to Port Hedland
was hot and cramped and slow
As we wiped the flies, from our eyes
all those years ago

And we've come so far, these past fifty years
We've come so far, with all our joy and all our tears
We've come so far, to be here today
to see the dream come true
And everyday's Australia Day

And now my little Sisters gotten married
I see her kids playing in the sun
And Mum and Dad, grandparents now
still living the dream that they begun
And me, well I might get lucky
find a girl and settle down
But I remember standing there
on a cold dark Southampton day
When my Daddy shared his dream …
you just took my breath away

And we've come so far, these past fifty years
We've come so far, with all our hopes and all our
fears
We've come so far, to be here today
To be a dream come true
And everyday's Australia Day
To be another dream come true
And everyday's Australia Day

Bibliography

Research and Resources

Considerable research has been done to provide accuracy of information, dates, names, events, etc.

Some resources are more anecdotal in nature, in the form of online blog posts or articles and their associated reader's comments, and may be the unsubstantiated recollection of people associated with events or places. Never-the-less, cross referencing of this type of data has revealed credible information, useful for this book.

References

Bath, Michael. "Tropical Cyclones." *Australian Severe Weather*. N.p., n.d. Web. 26 Sept. 2014. <http://www. australiasevereweather.com/cyclones/index.php>. Track tropical cyclones, hurricanes and typhoons for Australia and the Southern Hemisphere developed by Michael Bath.

Fremantle Ports. *Fremantle Passenger Terminal 50 Years Anniversary Booklet*. Fremantle, Western Australia: Fremantle Ports, 12 Dec. 2010. PDF. Fremantle Passenger Terminal, 50 Years. Celebrating its 50th anniversary in 2010, the Fremantle Passenger Terminal on Victoria Quay.

Goossens, Reuben. "Sitmar SS Fairsky - Piet Mulder

Sails on the SS Fairsky." *Sitmar SS Fairsky - Mulder Family*. SsMaritime, 2010. Web. 9 Aug. 2014. <http://ssmaritime.com/sitmar-mulder.htm>.

Hostel Manly. Perf. Cindy Dowden. YouTube. The Grove Library, 25 Oct. 2012. Web. 15 Oct. 2014. <http://www.youtube.com/watch?v=eWGF953R9Fs>.

Leisure Consultancy Services. *Needs Assessment, Concept Design and Implementation Plan for the Port Hedland Turf Club*. Rep. Port Hedland: Town of Port Hedland, 2012. Print.

Matheson, Julie. "History since 1896." *Port Hedland NOW*. Port Hedland NOW, Aug. 2010. Web. 6 Aug. 2014. <http://www.porthedlandnow.com.au/>. Julie is the daughter of Port Hedland Shire Councillor Colin Matherson.

Mikus, Pam. "Garylands: The Evolution of a Suburb." Thesis. Murdoch University, 2013. Print.

Museum Victoria. "Post World War II Migrant Ships: Fairsea." *Museum Victoria*. Museum Victoria, n.d. Web. 9 Sept. 2014. <http://museumvictoria.com.au/>. The Fairsea holds an important place in the memory of many immigrants to Australia during the post World War II period.

Outram, Trevor T. *This Is the Story of the Outram Family Who Emigrated from England in 1964. Port Hedland 1964 - 1970*. 2009. MS. Burleigh Heads, Australia.

Ports. "Port of Southampton to Port of Fremantle." *Ports*. <http://ports.com/sea-route/port-of-southampton,united-kingdom/port-of-fremantle-

perth,australia/>. Sea route map, distances,

Shire of Port Hedland. "Original Causeway; Wilson St. Port Hedland." *Heritage Council. State Heritage Office*. Government of Western Australia, 25 Jan. 2014. Web. 6 Sept. 2014. <http://stateheritage.wa.gov.au/>. Remains of seven mile causeway that connected the town of Port Hedland island

Skyring, Fiona. "The 1968–69 Introduction of Equal Wages for Aboriginal Pastoral Workers in the Kimberley." *National Museum of Australia*. National Museum of Australia, 10 Nov. 2009. Web. 13 Nov. 2014. <http://www.nma.gov.au/audio/transcripts/indig_part/NMA_1968_equal_wages_20091109.html>.

Town of Port Hedland, "Municipal Inventory of Heritage Places. Review," Laura Gray, Heritage & Conservation Consultant, 2007

Water and Rivers Commission. *Yule River Water Reserve Water Source Protection Plan*. Rep. no. WRP 30. Perth: Government of Western Australia, 2000. Print.

Wikipedia. Wikimedia Foundation, n.d. Web. 23 July 2014.

"Migrant Hostels Forum." *Migrant Hostels Forum*. MigrantWeb, 2003. Web. 5 Aug. 2014. <http://migrantweb.com/hostelsforum/>. Hostels were used to accomodate new Australians. 1950's - 1970's.

"Northam Army Camp Heritage Association Inc." *Northam Army Camp Heritage Association (NACHA)*. NACHA, 2010. Web. 6 Aug. 2014. <http://northamarmycamp.org.au/> Migrant centres in

Western Australia 1947-1963

"Ten Pound Pom." *Ten Pound Pom*. N.p., 2011. Web. 23 Oct. 2014. A social museum providing information about Australian migration history.

"Trove." *National Library of Australia*. Government of Australia, n.d. Web. 28 Sept. 2014. <http://trove.nla. gov.au/>. A collection of digitized newspaper articles, journals, diaries, letters, etc.

About The Author

Biography

Stephen Outram has a background of some eighteen years in architecture, and since 1997 has worked as a graphic artist, website developer and Internet consultant. More recently he is a writer and seminar presenter.

His family emigrated to Australia, from England in 1965, landing in Fremantle and spending five years in the northerly town of Port Hedland. In 1970 the family drove across the country from west to east and settled in Queensland's Gold Coast, where his parents and sister still reside. Educated in Queensland, Australia, Stephen studied at Brisbane's University of Technology in the early 1970s; he returned to study in 1995 at Dundee University, Scotland, achieving a Master of Science degree in Computing.

Stephen enjoys a diverse and wide range of projects including work, writing, music and song writing, boats and some sport. He is active with Surfrider Foundation Australia and is interested in sustainable and flourishing coastlines and waterways, free of plastics and pollution.

Visit the website for more information, stephenoutram. com

Other Books

By Stephen Outram

Wedding Speeches

For many, being asked to give a Wedding Speech is the first time they will speak to a larger group, and these speeches may be done only once in a lifetime. Copying and pasting someone else's lines off the Internet is just not good enough. This book will assist you in creating your speech, with ease!

Professional speaker and coach Stephen Outram connects you with everything you need, to accomplish what may be one of the most important speeches of your life!

- Discover a simple idea with 3 parts and begin organizing and preparing your Wedding Speech.

- How to convert what's in your head, into a vital resource.

- Detail descriptions of the 5 key wedding speeches, including the Bride's Speech—a woman's role in transforming long-standing traditions

- The real job of a wedding speech and your role in accomplishing it

- 9 things that you may have to handle that no one

tells you about!

Over 80 pages of information, ideas and techniques, designed to assist anyone who has been asked to give a Wedding Speech.

More information at stephenoutram.com

Dealers: Buying, Selling & Making Money

Dealers are people who can make things move! They are market creators and facilitate the flow of ideas, objects and objectives, connecting sellers and buyers. Dealers make money as a consequence of their ability to move energy and create results.

The ideas, concepts and tools that this book contains will connect you with the dealer that you have always wanted to be, but have not yet been introduced to; until now!

- What deals you will not walk away from that are costing you more than you know?

- The 5 key characters that you need, to be a dealer and make money.

- Are you speculating about making money rather than making money speculating?

- What is BIRGing and are you using it to disadvantage?

- Do your investments resemble losing football clubs that you loyally support with your money?

Treasure Hunter, Collector, Bargainer, Speculator and Investor—which are you using to your disadvantage and how do you turn that around?

More information at stephenoutram.com

Public Speaking: Beyond Fear

Public Speaking: Beyond Fear is designed for people who experience difficulty with public speaking and performance. It will also benefit people who think they have it all handled.

The ideas, concepts and tools contained in this book may catapult you to levels of freedom and ease with public speaking that you've never had before.

- Begin functioning beyond normal

- Discover why anxiety is your best friend

- The weird, hidden issues that you can change

- The Art of Public Speaking explained

- Understanding Fight-Flight and working with your body

- Why amateur speakers never get paid

What if your journey with public speaking was really an adventure, unfolding before you with each new choice you make?

More information at stephenoutram.com

Advanced Speaking Concepts

Advanced Speaking Concepts is written for people who are seeking to create something greater and something different with public speaking. It will also benefit people who are beginning; the new generation of speakers.

This book contains ideas and concepts to assist you going beyond all of the old, worn public speaking techniques that everyone else uses to be competent, average and safe.

- Exposed! The myth that public speaking is the No.1 fear.

- The weird and hidden issues that are holding you back.

- Nerves! Why you need them to perform better.

- Applause. A beginning, not the end.

- Manipulation! Using it to advantage.

What if your journey with public speaking was really an adventure unfolding before you with each new choice you make?

More information at stephenoutram.com

There's No Sex in Golf

With a glut of books available on Golf, how refreshing to see a book that is completely different. Author Stephen Outram, who has been playing the game since he was ten, explores the nooks and crannies many golfers normally ignore. Combining this with coaching examples, probing questions and some irreverent humour, it leaves a powerful mark in the golfing world.

Unlike most other golf books, *There's No Sex In Golf!* has little to say about your swing or what you need to fix or eliminate from your game. It asks you to add-to your game and create an abundance of choice, possibility and joy. Phrases like 'golf secrets' are the tools of those claiming they have the answer to your golf, but the facts are that until you are willing to stop competing to lose, none of it matters. Stephen Outram's *There's No Sex In Golf!* will assist you in a simple relaxed style so you will no longer be scratching your head about the 'secrets' of golf.

Life Beyond

Life Before is a collection of some twenty-six poems, musing and essays; written over a period of about ten years. Author, Stephen Outram, recalls how, "They shouted out at me. Enough of being hidden in the dusty dark drawer, they wanted out!" It's not so strange to consider that words have a life of their own and desire to be read. So here they are, twenty-six individual lives contributing their energy and presence to the creation of this book and asking you; "Will you read us?" Well, will you?

More information at stephenoutram.com